MAKE HER MINE

MEN IN CHARGE

TORY BAKER

Cover Design by LJ with Mayhem Cover Creations

Photographer by Sara Eirew with Sara Eirew Photography

Editor Julia Good with Diamond in the Rough Editing

❀ Created with Vellum

To anyone that lived a life they thought was perfect, until it wasn't.

PLAYLIST

Make Her Mine Playlist

You, Me, and Whiskey- Justin Moore
Stoned- Parker McCollum
Tears the Size of Texas- Ben Burgess
Rock and A Hard Place- Bailey Zimmerman
Flower Shops- ERNEST
Daylight- Watchhouse
Space and Time- S.G. Goodman
Why- Read Southall Band
Proud Mary- Tina Turner
Just Like Leaving- Bella White
So Low- Koe Wetzel
Dirty Looks- Lainey Wilson
Heart Like A Truck-Lainey Wilson
Watermelon Moonshine- Lainey Wilson

Mr. Saturday Night- Jon Pardi
From a Lover's Point of View- Zach Bryan

BLURB

She was always the one who got away.

Rosaleigh caught my eyes from the beginning, but I didn't make my move.
She was too young.
Unfortunately, my best friend didn't have the same morals.
It killed me, watching from a distance as he disrespected the woman who was always meant to be mine.

When she finally discovers the truth about him, all bets are off.
I'm done holding back.
I make my move, ready to prove she has a real man now— one who will have her back and give her the life she deserves.

I won't let anything stop me.

She's not getting away again.

I'm going to make her mine.

This is the first book in the Men in Charge series, each book will be a complete stand alone, the common denominator? An alpha Hero, a man that goes after what he wants, a guaranteed happily ever after, and of course steamy romance!

PROLOGUE

Rosaleigh

Ten Months Earlier

"HEY, GIRLS, WHERE'S YOUR FATHER?" I ask as I walk through the door. All the lights are off, minus the small lamp in the corner of the room. David's patrol car wasn't in the driveway, and neither was our second vehicle. Both of our daughters have blonde hair and a similar build to mine, minus the fact that one is my height while the other isn't that far off, with eyes that are like looking at my own; only theirs are red and bloodshot, as if they've been crying on the couch, huddled together, a rarity these days. They're usually at each other's throats, especially in the morning when Rory is taking her sweet time on her hair and mascara while all Emmy wants to do is brush her teeth, run a comb through her hair, and call it a day. That's when the arguments start and I have to wade in, unless David is home. Then the house is as quiet as a tomb, no one willing to wake him up if he's been working the nightshift.

"He's gone," my oldest daughter, Rory, who's on the cusp of womanhood in the form of being a teenager, states. She'll be thirteen in a few short weeks. Time has flown by, and that saying 'Time is a thief' couldn't be more accurate. It feels like only yesterday when I admitted to myself that at the ripe age of fifteen, I was pregnant, a baby having a baby. It's then I notice Emmy is practically on top of Rory, cuddled into her side, the tip of her thumb in her mouth, a habit she's had forever but rarely uses unless a time calls for it, usually when she's overtired, upset, or nervous. Tonight, it looks to be a combination of all three.

"What do you mean, he's gone?" I ask, stepping out of my shoes, dropping my bag to the floor, and walking closer until I'm sitting in front of them, ass to the wooden coffee table, unable to understand that short sentence. Rory's lip quivers, Emmy has tears in her eyes, and my stomach, well, my stomach plummets to my feet.

"He's gone, Mommy." I'm trying to wrap what those words mean around my head, David, my husband, their father, is a cop in small town of Abalee, Georgia. The place where David was born and raised. Me, not so much. I was a transplant from one of the many places my mom decided to up and move on a moment's notice. Before moving here, home was a joke. We never stayed in one place for longer than a year because whoever the boyfriend or husband of the month my mom was after would be in another town, giving her the opportunity to quit paying rent on one apartment and leaving before getting evicted for her to do it all over again, a never-ending cycle. They say that history has a chance of repeating itself when it comes to you being a product of your youth. I may have been a statistic in some ways when it came to being a teen mother like my own was, but that's where the similarities ended. A cycle I'm glad that I'm no longer a part of. "I'm still not understanding, sweetheart. Was daddy hurt at work? Is he in the hospital?" I work at the local plant nursery part-time, not wanting to lose my identity as a cop's wife and a stay-at-home mother. Believe me, with my own mother and her vocal wishes of wanting to live off a man, I made sure I always had some semblance of independence.

"No, I don't think so," Rory murmurs, confusion cloying the air. The pinch of her eyebrows worries me even more.

"Baby, I can't help either of you or your father if I don't know what's happening." Emmy takes that moment to fly into my arms. Her small gangly body wraps around mine like an octopus. She's all arms and legs, still growing into herself. A thing of beauty with her carefree ways. God, I love my girls more than they'll ever understand.

"Mommy, he left. A call came in, and he left. Da-Dad, he said he was leaving and not coming back, that he was sorry, then he walked out," Emmy says out loud the words Rory couldn't speak. Their personalities are like night and day.

Emmy lives to talk, while Rory is the one who looks but doesn't say what she's thinking, not until the words are perfectly formed.

"Shh, it's okay, sweetheart. I'm sure it was work. He'll call or something, okay?" This is so unlike David. Even if he had to go undercover for work, he'd tell me. He wouldn't describe the case or how long he'd be gone, just that he might be unavailable, that the documents were in the safe, how the force would take care of his girls should something happen, and that he was carrying us with him. The last time that happened was years ago, when the girls were toddlers, not now, and to leave like this without saying goodbye or talking. It's unimaginable.

"Mom, it wasn't work. Dad was as white as a sheet of paper," Rory says, still sitting on the couch. My hand wanders to hers, clasping it in mine. I know the state she's in right now, hugging her would be out of the question.

"I'll call Nix. He'll know something. He always does." Phoenix "Nix" Drakos, David's best friend, my girls' godfather, and all-around great guy. Truth be told, he's the man who most strive to be but can't attain, and lucky for us, he's right across the street.

"I don't think Dad is coming back, Mom." Emmy's tears leak against my shoulder as her emotions overflow. And me, well, I'm at a loss for words. Never in our thirteen-year relationship did I think David would be capable of making me second-guess every single thing we've built in our life.

Except that's exactly what he does.

1

ROSALEIGH

P resent Day

"UGH, this year can just fuck right off." My lungs hurt, and my chest is heaving. The pillow covering my face really isn't helping, but it was scream into that or into thin air. I'm pretty sure the neighborhood, as well as my two daughters, wouldn't take too kindly to that. Not that I don't have an excuse; I do. I'm not putting that mildly either. Our life has been left in tatters. Do my girls know the truth? Sadly, yes they do. David, the man I thought I knew with every depth of my being, screwed his own family over. When the girls and I walk down the small local streets, pity is marring the faces of people we've known forever. I guess it's better than a look of betrayal. Oh, that would be so very fitting. Lump us into the same pile of shit that is David. That's not the case, though. Having the chief of police knock on your door the same night your girls are falling apart at the seams, not understanding a single thing, will do that to you.

The pieces of our life are now in the trash, right along with my love for David. It's gone. Destroyed. Finito. We were young; I was younger by four years. That's how the story goes with a lot of the now adults from our youth. Your number one goal was to get married, have two point four children, a white picket fence around a modest one-story house, and a dog. At the time, it was the absolute best thing that could ever happen to me. I was born to be a mother—I know that like the back of my hand. My childhood was chaos, full of abandonment and strings where love was concerned. I never, ever wanted my own kids to go through that. And for the most part, my girls haven't. Chaos, yes, because wrestling two girls, each in a different stage of their life, is hard. That didn't matter to me, though. Running around, getting the girls ready for school, toting them around, both at a different school with a different schedule, I thrived on it. Add into Rory being the track superstar she is, while Emmy does ballet and dance, it was no wonder after I'd drop into bed exhausted, mentally, emotionally, the moment my eyes slammed shut, I was sleeping. A coping mechanism of sorts. It was either that or wine, and at this moment in time, turning to alcohol would be stupid. My girls already lost one parent; they don't need to lose another one.

It's months later, and I still have moments where I'm lost to an emotional upheaval. The girls are in their after-school activities, and I have a rare afternoon off from work now that I work full-time at the nursery. So, I came home and decided to have a meltdown. It seemed like an okay time to do it. Not that I can schedule to cry in the shower, with two young girls and only one full bathroom in the house. One or the other is constantly barging in. It's Grand freaking Central Station, with gossip on the latest comings and goings of who's dating whom, which boy Rory thinks is cute, how she's got a B in one class, and is freaking out about not having straight A's. I wish I had the drive she does at her age; I was more worried about making sure not to become my mother. Sadly, that kind of happened when I landed pregnant at the same age she did. Emmy, though, she'd come in and ask me to help with some kind of art and craft, if she thought it was okay to start shaving her legs at the age of ten. I choose my battles wisely. If she wanted to do something like that, it was up to her. I only reminded her that once she started, it was an uphill battle.

I'm still in shock that the man I gave my heart, my body, and so much of my life was this rotten. That's what the head-lines read. *Dirty Cop of Abalee a Wanted Fugitive.* Yep, David is still running from the law. Seizing illegal drugs only to funnel them back to the cartel is a bit of an issue in the eyes of the law. The police chief didn't go into too many details, seeing as how it was an open investigation. He asked if I knew his whereabouts, to work with him, which would be awesome if I did. It was the other agencies that were complete assholes. A shiver runs up my body as I remember the days that followed. David's disappearance left me with a pile of horse shit to wade through, that's for sure, with two girls in the throes of teenage life while not knowing how to handle how angry I am at him for putting us through this alone, plus one less income. Thankfully, we kept the first house we purchased years after we got married, so the mortgage isn't steep. It still isn't cheap. My car is not paid off either, and my credit is shot to shit now that things have gone haywire. Thank you, David. My credit cards were cut off, too. It was either pay them or put food on the table, which was an easy choice when two growing girls were involved.

"Fucking, fuck, fuck!" I scream into my pillow-covered face one last time before I need to put this pity party to rest. I have to throw dinner together and go do the round of pickups. On weekday afternoons I don't have off, David's parents step in. They are literal saints compared to their son. It's not their fault; they didn't raise him that way. They gave that man everything, and not in a spoiled kind of way either. He had a roof over his head, a loving family who supported him, and dinner around the table every night. And while I can't do all those things now that I'm working full-time, as soon as I get them on the bus, I rush off to work at Minnie's Nursery Center in my gas-guzzling SUV. Another thing on my to-do list: trade that beast in for something smaller as well as getting rid of the payment. That would help tremendously. A pipe dream is what it is. Did I mention David left me with all the debt—cars, house, and credit cards? If only I could plant my fist in his face right about now.

Before meeting David, I was on track to go to nursing school, a straight-A student ready to start college. That all changed, of course. When I look back, it's okay that things evolve. I wouldn't trade my girls for the world. I would, however, change the timing in which I had them. Alright, to be fair, we probably should have planned things differently. Me working two jobs while pregnant to put his needs before mine probably wasn't smart, but at the time, it was different. If I had to do things over, I'd change that. David's career to become a cop was put first, especially after an unplanned pregnancy occurred.

Here I am, nearly thirteen years later, with our two girls and doing it all on my own. While he's where? Nowhere to be seen, literally. His phone is off, can't even be pinged, and he's got no social media. The only reason I'm still paying for his stupid phone line is in case the good cops catch a break. Bleeding hearts unite. I freaking swear other than that, it's like he was never here, besides leaving three girls consumed by not understanding.

The ringing of the doorbell makes me get up from my bed before I'm actually ready to. Just because the pity party is over, doesn't mean a woman can't rest. "Just a minute!" I call out, grumbling while I move through the empty house.

"Hurry up, woman, it's cold as balls out here," I hear a man's voice on the other side of the door. That would be David's best friend, Phoenix, the man who seems to hate my future ex-husband as much as I do. All while being here for us every step of the way. Leaky faucet? Nix to the rescue. Rory can't figure out her math homework, you guessed it. Nix is there to help. Emmy needs help with new ballet shoes? Nix again. I seriously think I fell in love with the wrong guy, because all of a sudden, the feelings I have for David's friend, well, they aren't so friendly anymore.

2

NIX

I shouldn't be on her doorstep, yet here I fucking am, bags of groceries in hand. Rory sent me a text asking if I could make them dinner tonight, something I don't get to do a lot of, seeing as how I'm working six days a week at my auto repair shop. Usually, it's the other way round. Leigh is making me dinner as a thank-you for picking up where Douchebag David fucked up.

"Jesus, it's a good thing the girls aren't around. Talking about balls might get you kicked in them." Rosaleigh opens the door, mouth full of sass, pouty lips, long blonde hair down in her signature natural waves when she's home. It's a damn good thing the girls took after their mother, too. David, that worthless piece of shit, deserves no part of Rosaleigh, Rory, or Emmy.

"I'd like to see them try. Rory texted." I lift the bag of groceries up to show her the reason I'm here, inviting myself in as I take a step inside the foyer.

"That girl, I swear. Souvlaki?" she asks as she turns around. Her ass is in a pair of skintight jeans, an ass I should not be looking at but do just the same.

"Yep, said she needed it, or she would die. Her exact words." The girl might be quiet and stoic to some, but when Rory lets her guard down, drops, the wall, and she lets you in, with it comes her flare for the dramatics.

"She's probably over eating sandwiches, no matter how creative I've gotten. Joke's on her because I was going to actually cook tonight. I'm not going to argue with your dinner, though. I'd be a fool." I chuckle. It's not a hardship to take care of the James women, especially their mother.

"You talk to Ophelia lately?" I ask. My baby sister was pissed when Rosaleigh didn't call her to talk about David, and it was me on the phone. I busted her chops, explaining to her Leigh was a bit busy fielding calls from news people while dealing with the fallout. We both knew that fucker wasn't good enough for her, even in high school. David and I were seniors when Rosaleigh and my sister came up as freshmen. I kept to myself. She was younger, my sister's age, and no way was I going to fuck around and find out. David didn't have the same care for her that I did. She was barely a junior in high school when David swooped in at nineteen years old to her fifteen. Her mom, another worthless piece of shit, was gone more often than not. If roles were reversed, and I was Rory and Emmy's father and some dumb fuck was sniffing around a girl who was four years younger than her, my fist would be a permanent fixture in his face. Even though Rosaleigh was like a second daughter to my parents, they couldn't talk any sense into her. That's also when we figured it all out; she was locked to David in a permanent way. It took my dad putting me in a headlock, whispering that if I fucked him up, it'd be me in jail, not him. What good would that do to anyone? David and I had words, not the brotherly kind either. Rosaleigh was beautiful back then, is even more gorgeous today, but to be so stupid as to fuck up her future, being saddled with a dick like him, it didn't sit right with me. I threatened to kick his ass if he didn't stick around and make things right.

"She doesn't complain about that. I'm assuming it's a craving." I arch my eyebrow. It must click into place because she's turning around, moving to the side of the fridge, and checking the calendar.

"Shit. I better start making brownies while you cook souvlaki. I love my daughter, you know that as well as I do, but her need for chocolate is fierce when it's, well, yeah, that time," Rosaleigh responds while I set the bags down on the kitchen counter and take all of the ingredients out. This will take a while to get going—making the marinade for the pork and the fresh tzatziki. The only thing I wouldn't attempt to make is the pita bread. My mother being the amazing woman she is had me covered when I told her I was stopping at the store for Rory's favorite meal, saying the grocery is crap and she made hers fresh that day.

"Like mother, like daughter. Mom said to stop by her house this week. She's got something for you." Mom didn't elaborate, and I didn't ask.

"It won't be until the weekend. I'm working the rest of the week except for Sunday." Leigh starts getting her dessert ready while I do my own thing beside her. The two of us have become accustomed to nights like these. Since I live across the street, popping in here and there isn't abnormal. The girls banging on my door isn't either.

"She won't mind. You wanna talk about why your door was unlocked already when you opened it?" I ask. I know she has a bad habit of not locking up after herself, seeing as how the door is revolving when Rory and Emmy are home. That doesn't mean I'm not going to stay on top of them to be smart. There are too many sickos out there, and the fight that is about to happen, let's just say it's one of many.

"I forgot." She shrugs her shoulders, defeated. I'm unimpressed with where this conversation is going. I wash my hands and dry them off. Now that the meat is cut and marinating, I'll wait for the girls to get home before I cook it.

"You forgot?" I lean my hip against the counter, arms crossed over my chest, pissed as fuck at her negligence. David is in the fucking wind, stealing drugs for a damn cartel, and here she is, forgetting to lock the damn doors.

"That's what I said." Leigh won't look at me, her eyes on the task at hand, further ticking me off. And I bet if I went to her bedroom window, I'd find it unlocked and cracked, too.

"I'm coming over this weekend. Leave me a set of keys. The lock's being changed so it'll engage once the door shuts. You and the girls will have a code, and you can see who attempts to use it with an app. I should have fucking done that after shit went down." I'm hoping she'll give me that fiery attitude of hers, so I can enjoy Leigh spitting mad, but it doesn't come. Instead, she locks her shit down.

"Whatever. Just tell me what it costs." The dark circles around her eyes, the hunching of her shoulders, and the tank top she's wearing that once hugged her figure but is now slipping off her frame tell me exactly where she is mentally and emotionally. Yeah, Ophelia and my mom will have to do something, and soon, if she doesn't get out of this funk. To say I wasn't David's friend any longer is putting it lightly. In fact, it was shortly after the two of them got married that I severed our friendship. Rosaleigh didn't know it. It was an unspoken rule between David and me that while we were no longer tight like we once were, there was no reason for me to stay away from the girls. Rosaleigh may not have seen what he was, but I could see through his bullshit from a mile away.

"Not worried about the money." I wave her off. She crosses her arms underneath her tits, making my gaze move from her eyes to her chest as she mirrors my stance, and I have a hard time forcing my eyes back up to hers.

"Phoenix, you've paid for enough around here. I promise I'm back on my feet, and if I need help, I'll ask, okay?" I don't want to add more shit to her plate.

"Alright." My house across the street was once my parents', and I know for a fact Rosaleigh put her foot down when she wanted the house she's in now. David wanted to be closer to his parents, but Leigh wanted to be closer to mine. It caused a battle, but she stood her ground and said take it or leave it. A year or so ago, my parents were ready to move into a smaller home closer to the water. I made them an offer, and I've been living across the street ever since. Lucky me, and I don't mean that in a bad way, not when I'm busy trying to mend not one but three broken hearts.

3

ROSALEIGH

"Oh my God, I'm starving. Nix is the absolute best." Rory walks in the door, energetic as ever. A smile takes over my face when the best parts of me walk in.

"You're hungry, girlfriend; I am famished, and Nix makes the best ever dinner. Sorry, not sorry, Mom." Emmy, never to be outdone in the dramatic department, makes everyone aware of her stance on the subject.

"And what do we say about dinner to Nix?" I pop the brownies in the oven to bake, knowing Phoenix will use the grill outside for the souvlaki. The girls live for the skewered meat, and to be honest, not having to cook, only having to worry about dessert, is an honest to God blessing.

"Thanks, Nix!" Emmy exclaims while she drops her backpack right by the front door for anyone to trip over as they try to leave the house, namely the man who's taking care of dinner. I give her a pointed look. She rolls her eyes. Typical preteen behavior, but she grabs the bag and places it on the hook where it's supposed to go.

"No problem, kiddo. Don't let Ya-Ya hear you say that about dinner. She'll box your ears," Nix replies, a grin on his face. He's not wrong. His mother is a force to be reckoned with. She's also the best woman I know, taking me under her wing when David and I first came home with Rory, then adding to our family a few years later. She swooped right in. It was hard to see them move out of their home that gave me more memories than my own family did. The only good part was the Greek god, yep, that's me casting a lingering gaze toward my husband's best friend, which reminds me, I really need to see an attorney about divorcing that ass. I make mental note to ask Nix if he knows who I should see, preferably not in Abalee. The townspeople are sweet, didn't judge me for being saddled with David and his machinations. That doesn't mean they didn't talk. The girls felt the brunt of it more than me. David's parents even worse. I feel for them. Really, I do. And just because I'm divorcing David, doesn't mean I'll be divorcing them.

"Speaking of, don't make any plans Sunday. We're going to see Ya-Ya and Papou if they'll be home." Rory walks around the kitchen peninsula to squeeze Nix. He kisses the top of her head, whispering something I can't hear. Then she moves toward me to give me a hug.

"You got it, Mamacita." Rory's in her second year of Spanish, and it's translating into our home life wherever she sees fit. She's older beyond her years, even before things went sideways. Rory is doing everything in her power to get ahead in any and all of her schoolwork. She's even talking about taking online classes between her eighth and ninth grade year during her summer break. All so she can achieve her dream of becoming a pediatric cardiologist, a goal she's been set on because of Ophelia, who is not only Nix's sister but also my best friend, even if she is living that jet-set life of hers. Anyways, when Rory was little, Ophelia and she would watch all the fiction and non-fiction shows pertaining to life in the medical field. The Drakos family became mine, as well as David's parents, though it was strained back then; it's nothing compared to what it is now. So, I decided to quit going to the local high school once I started showing my pregnancy bump, enrolled in college to finish out my last year and receive my diploma. Of course, life liked to derail me a bit. Morning sickness that lasted all day made it impossible to finish in the timeframe I wanted to. After Rory came along, Ophelia and Nix's parents would watch my little girl, I'd go to school, and when I came home, those two would be snuggled on the couch watching television. It didn't stop there. When I was working, that's where you'd find the two of them. Ophelia was never too busy for her girls; she still isn't.

"I'll take you girls. I'm going there anyways. May as well take one vehicle instead of two," Nix says. "Now, who's helping with the vegetables and tzatziki?" I wrinkle my nose, knowing their affinity for grilled onions, something I don't like, along with mushrooms. Those two items they can have.

"I will," Emmy says,

"Not me. Can you make a pot of coffee? I have a lot of

homework." I roll my eyes. I never make her a pot of coffee when she pulls 'all-nighters'. Her version of those is passing out by ten o'clock.

"I do not, probably because I'm the smarter one and don't try to kill myself with schoolwork," Emmy says. Little turkey that she is, while she may not be taking her classes early like Rory, she's still in hard classes.

"Ugh, speaking of. Nix, can you help me after dinner?" Rory asks. She places her backpack on the chair at the kitchen table and unzips it, pulling out her school laptop, a book, and notebook, as well as her pencil pouch.

"Math again?" He looks at Rory then Emmy, giving them his full attention. Not for the first time in my life do I feel like I chose the wrong man along the way. David had his faults; we all do, but maybe I kept my rose-colored glasses on a little too much for a little too long. I didn't think anything of working two jobs while he attended the academy to make sure our bills were paid. As long as we had a roof over our head, food in our bellies, and we could pay some money to Ya-Ya for watching Rory, I was happy. It was our little family of three until we added Emmy into the mix. David had been on the force for a year by that time. I went down to working part-time and worked around his shifts, and when the house we're in now came on the market, I knew it would be ours, no matter how much David wanted to live closer to his parents. The Drakos were my family back then, and they still are now. I wanted to have them near, plus it's not like we could afford a house in his parents' neighborhood at the time, and definitely not now in the shape I'm in.

"It's stupid, Nix. It's like my teacher thinks we're mathematicians and can learn college geometry without her, you know, actually teaching us in a way we can understand, which would be more than nice." Nix being Nix listens to her, a smile tugging at his lips. I notice that he's letting his beard grow in more, and a new tattoo has been added to his sleeve. Yeah, I am noticing entirely too much about Phoenix Drakos, including his muscular build, tight ass, and even firmer thighs that are encased in worn-in denim.

"Sweetheart, I hate to tell you this, but the career you're choosin', there's gonna be a shit ton of math involved." Nix's choice of words doesn't bother me, probably because when I'm pissed, I cuss like a sailor. David was even worse than me, so while it might not be what their grandparents would like on both sides, Nix's and David's, it is what it is.

"I know, I know. Maybe I'll have a better teacher in high school?" I laugh low in my throat. Oh, to be that hopeful teenager again. Rory looks at me, rolls her eyes, and huffs out a breath.

"Doubtful. Apologize to your mom. I'll cook dinner, then we'll see what we can work out." Another quality in Nix that has me thinking about things I shouldn't. I wouldn't have said a word, a battle that I didn't have the energy to deal with.

"Sorry, Momsies." The attitude is put away and she moves toward me, arms open. I do the same. Hugs are rare these days, so I'll take every single one I can get.

"I want in!" Emmy barrels into our hug. My arms wrap around my girls as my eyes close for a moment, soaking it all in, and when the girls have had their fill of mom time, Nix has that look on his face, the one that has his jaw tightening as if he's pissed off at something or somebody. He's never willing to talk about it, and I'm too much of a ninny to open that can of worms.

4

NIX

"Emmy, Rory, if you don't get your butts out this door, we're going to be late for school and I'm going to be late for work. That means eating cereal, Ramen, and peanut butter sandwiches." I'm heading into work at the same time she's trying to get the girls out the door, a task in itself. Leigh must be feeling generous because any other day, they'd be on the bus. That or they're running late. I look down at my phone, noticing the time, and I'd say the girls overslept this morning, seeing as how they're usually gone before me.

"That's not fair! Unless it's your French toast peanut butter sandwiches." Emmy comes flying out the door, backpack on, lunch bag in her hand, flinging her hair with her unoccupied hand.

"I'll take that into consideration with management, meaning me. Rory Michelle, let's roll." I'm trying not to laugh. The woman has a heart of gold, is stronger than anyone I know, including my own mother. We're not going to tell her that. I'd be on her shit list until the end of time.

"Madre, I'm sorry, I'm sorry." Rory is a flustered mess. It's becoming her usual with the load she seems to willingly carry. I hate to say it, but the girl and math do not jive whatsoever. There's only so much you can do. The rest is going to be up to her.

"Let's go, let's go. Apology accepted." That's Rosaleigh, the woman I let slip through my fingers, standing on the sidelines like a second-string quarterback waiting for his time to shine. Fucking David James, my childhood best friend. That all changed the second he figured out how his dick worked. A subject I won't even touch. If the conversation came out and Leigh asked point blank, I'd fucking lie. That woman has been through too much in her lifetime. There's no damn need to add fuel to the fire.

"Nix! Good morning!" Emmy, who was waiting for her mother to unlock the door to the black Tahoe she drives, starts to take off toward me.

"Good morning, Emmy, Rory, Leigh." I know there's no stopping Emmy, and if Rosaleigh is late for work, well, that won't do.

"Hey, Nix, thanks for helping me last night," Rory says with a yawn.

"Morning. We've got to go. I have to open the nursery, and these two knuckleheads slept through their alarm." I arch an eyebrow. I'm pretty sure the two younger girls weren't the only ones. "Fine, whatever. So did I."

"Girls, head to my truck. No need for your mom to be late. You okay with that?" It's an afterthought, really. Probably should have made sure she was okay with it. Rosaleigh's tell is chewing on her bottom lip, teeth indenting it. If the girls weren't here, I'd let me thoughts run wild thinking about all the things her lips, tongue, and teeth could be doing to me right about now.

"Life saver. I owe you one. Though, I don't know how I can ever repay you." Rosaleigh waves both of her hands, fanning her eyes. Jesus, it's one of those weeks for her, it seems. Though, I'm not commenting a single word, knowing if Rory is hitting that time of the month, Rosaleigh might be right behind her. Shit, once it happens to Emmy, I'm fucked. There won't be enough chocolate in Abalee to handle the James women.

"Tell your mom goodbye. Leigh, we'll talk later, okay? I've got time today, so I'm going to work on replacing your locks." My hand cups her jaw, thumb sliding over her cheek, doing more than I ever have in the ten months since douchebag David has been gone.

"Bye, Momma," Rory says, chasing after Emmy, who just waves over her shoulder. The two of them will fight over riding shot gun, and I'll wade in as soon as I make sure their mom is okay.

"You good?" Leigh doesn't say anything. My hand remains where it is, giving her the time she needs to regain her composure as she closes her eyes. A tear leaks down her cheek, and my thumb swipes through the moisture. Not for the first time am I seeing just how tired she is. The façade she shows to the outside world slips when I'm around, allowing herself to be more vulnerable. I hate that she's going through this alone. It's one thing if the man you've known and loved your whole life dies for a cause, but to find out everything you thought you ever knew was a lie, that he left you and your two girls to pick up the pieces, it's a whole new low.

"No. I will be, though." She takes a deep breath. My cock twitches as I watch her chest move up, then down, unable to avert my eyes when I notice her nipples pebble beneath her shirt.

"Fuck yeah, you will. Get to work. We'll talk later, when the girls actually go to sleep." If Rory and Emmy didn't have their noses pressed up against the windows of the truck, I'd dip my head toward hers, feel those soft lips against mine, and finally fucking taste the woman I crave. Neither of the girls argued about the front seat, apparently.

"Thanks, Nix." Her eyes open. Gone is the sadness that was just there. Now there's a look of determination.

"Always here, sweetheart. Now, get your ass to work. I've got the girls. I'll grab a bottle of wine for tonight." This time, I dip my knees. Our height difference makes it impossible for us to be on eye level, and right now, looking at her hazel eyes is what I need.

"Alright." Rosaeleigh's hand goes on top of mine, squeezing it in a reassuring way that she's good with me helping take the load off her back today.

"Later, Leigh." It's hard to walk away, but this time I know I'll be walking back to her, and it'll be for good.

"I swear, Rosaleigh Michelle James, sometimes I think you married the wrong man." I'm halfway down the driveway when I hear her mumbled words. Jesus, this woman has no idea what she does to me. There's nothing I can do right now for her to see it either, and now that I've made it my mission to take the girls to school, which I know will include stopping to get donuts, coffee for myself and Rory—hers more of a sugary sweet concoction and lower on the caffeine factor—and juice for Emmy, it'll have to wait. Then I'll get the guys started at the shop I own, Drakos Auto Shop. It was once my dad's, handed down to me with a steep price tag. One I willingly paid because he and Mom were ready to retire. I only have a few appointments on the books today, which works in my favor seeing as there's a need to hit the hardware store for Rosaleigh's house, and I'm adding stopping at the store to grab her a bottle of her favorite Pinot Noir.

"Finally. I'm starving. Donuts?" Emmy asks the second I open the door to my truck.

"Coffee, please?" Rory adds to it. What did I say? The girls know I'm not going to say no. Plus, I see Rosaleigh, working her ass off on every day that ends with *y*, and it's a rare occasion if they eat outside of the house. That includes the diner in town, fast food, or going to eat at a nice restaurant.

"On one condition." I get situated in the driver's seat, start up the truck, and turn the radio down so I don't bust our eardrums with the heavy rock I was listening to on the way home last night.

"Don't tell Mom!" Rory and Emmy say in unison,

followed by laughter. If Rosaleigh were to know about all the times I've taken them for donuts in the morning and milkshakes in the afternoon, it would create an argument where she feels compelled to pay me back even though we both know that would break the bank even more. So, for the time being, this will be our secret.

5

ROSALEIGH

I came home and was locked out of my own house. Yep, that was not the welcome home I was expecting, and had I not just paid the mortgage, I probably would have worried about something entirely different. Yes, I know the bank will hound you until you make the payment, but that doesn't negate the fact that this single mother of two girls is dead on her feet. When I went to work this morning, I had no idea I'd be opening and closing the nursery, essentially working twelve hours. I was unprepared, to say the least. The lunch I packed the night before in the form of leftovers is now in my hand, long forgotten when Minnie called me stating that not only did she have the flu, but so did Derek, our other employee.

The weird part about this equation is that Nix's truck isn't in the driveway. Rory texted me earlier saying he was picking them up from their extracurricular activities and they'd see me at home. Which means they should be here, at least starting on their homework, since it's seven o'clock at night. That saying, the lights are on, but nobody's home. It really hits me right now as I walk around the house, noticing just about every freaking light is on in the house. Never do I leave the house with a light on, minus the one above the stove. Bills aren't cheap, especially the electric bill. Luck is on my side because I know for a fact that my bedroom window is unlocked. Yeah, yeah, leaving windows unlocked isn't smart. I can hear Nix now giving me all kinds of shit about it. Needless to say, I never heed his warnings, which is why my hands are pressed against the glass, sliding it up an inch at a time. Damn my body for being on the shorter side for a female. Five foot and four inches is not tall when your teenager and preteen are slowly looming over your stature.

"Jackpot," I say to the quiet surrounding me. The only noise are the trees swaying with the subtle breeze, crickets and frogs croaking. Our neighborhood is on the older side, most of the houses built in the fifties. Some of the houses have additions built, and some have been remodeled, taking away the old-world charm. My house is not one of them. The only things that've been upgraded are the windows, doors, and flooring. There was no knocking walls down for an open floor plan. The kitchen was already open enough; no need to turn it into some modern work of art that would never fit the home. Once I have the window open, making sure it's completely up and won't fall back down, I use every ounce of muscle in my body to lift myself up, making it until I'm doing a teeter-totter, my stomach taking the brunt of it.

"Stupid short arms. Stupid short legs." I kick my legs, trying to gain some momentum to move my body off the ledge to get inside. If I'd have only used my phone, maybe called one of the girls, and yes, my ten-year-old has a phone. Sue me. We all have such a crazy busy life that adding a phone to the mix has helped, plus I can track either of them at any given time. For that matter, they can track me, which they do all the damn time, except maybe for tonight.

"What in the actual fuck?" I lift my head, making my whole body do this weird wibble-wobble action. I lose whatever traction I did have, causing me to slide backwards. Damn this body of mine.

"Shit, shit, shit," I sputter out. My head drops down, hands grasping at thin air, knowing there's nothing or no way to break the fall that's clearly about to happen. God, if my girls followed Nix into my room, had their phones with them, there's not a single doubt in my mind they'd be videoing my shenanigans. And the first person they'd send it to is Ophelia, followed by Ya-Ya and Papou. Though, the last two members of the family would need help on how to watch the video.

"Jesus, Leigh, are you trying to kill yourself?" That air I was grasping at becomes Nix's firm shoulders, the tips of my fingers pressing in, unconsciously, as he prevents me from falling to my near death. I mean Nix did use the words *kill yourself,* so I'd say it's okay to be a teeny bit dramatic. What I'm not expecting is the way he continues to hold me, my chest pressed against his body, my nipples pebbling in a way that I try not to admit even to myself only seems to happen with the Greek god present, or when I'm thinking about him in the still of the night. What I'm not expecting is to feel something thick and heavy pressed into my lower stomach.

A hiss of air escapes his lips, or the fact that it's me sinking closer to Nix.

I never did respond to his question, and right now doesn't seem like the time to do so either. In fact, judging by the way he's looking at me—tongue sliding along his lower lip as my eyes trace the movement, my core clenching, panties soaked like only Nix seems to do—I'd say right now is definitely not the time to question anything other than my sanity. This isn't smart, right? He's my future ex-husband's best friend. There's some forbidden bro code you don't cross, right? Or am I making that up and it's more of a sisterhood thing, like the sisters before misters.

"You wanna tell me why you couldn't use the front door to your own home?" Nix breaks the silence as well as the tension.

"I tried to open the door. It was locked. The lights were on, but I didn't see anyone. It's not like your truck was in your driveway. I figured the girls were with you somewhere, and I knew the window was unlocked, so why bother calling or texting?" I state it as a question instead of a statement as I attempt to step out of his grasp. Nix isn't allowing it, though. If anything, his hands grip my hips tighter, holding me hostage in his arms. Only I'm not really putting up a fight if he were to kidnap me.

"Truck's at the shop. Swapped it for the car because Rory asked if she could help me work on it, and instead of taking her to the shop, figured it'd be better to be home when she gets bored. Emmy's already discussing how Rory's going to ask for latex gloves in order to change the fluids." That sounds about right with both girls. "The girls and I were out back, grilling. Your wine is on the counter. And the reason you don't know the code is because I'm not texting it," Nix states, dark hair messy from what I'm sure is him running his fingers through it, cerulean-blue eyes on me, and his lips... Jesus, there's something wrong with me. His lips, they look pillowy soft. My mind is going in every which direction. How'd they feel pressed against my own, wondering what he'd do with them if they traveled along my skin, and then there's that one place in mind I try to never to go to. The memo is lost in translation because suddenly, instead of my fingers working my clit, it's Nix's mouth on my pussy. Fucked, that's what I am, and not in the way I'm craving to be either. Oh no, I'd much rather be on my hands and knees, in the bed, on the couch, the floor. It doesn't really matter as long as Nix is behind me, both of us are naked, his hand wrapped around the strands of my hair, pulling my head back as his other one grips my hip enough to leave bruises as he fucks his cock in and out of my wet center.

"You keep looking at me like that, Leigh, something's going to happen you're not expecting." Nix chooses that time to interrupt the fantasy that's working through mind, making me shelve it for now, knowing damn well I'll be using it for my spank bank material tonight.

"Oh." It comes out like more of a purr. My head drops, eyes close. Hello, embarrassment city.

"We're gonna come back to that, and soon." His hand moves from its place on my lower back, sliding up the length of my spine until he's massaging beneath my hair. I place my forehead on his chest, unable to resist the moment where I'm in someone's arms, someone I'm not related to, and what else is a woman to do when she smells the unique scent of Phoenix Drakos, a spicy mix of oranges and spruce, along with undercurrents of oil from his day at the shop?

"Not tonight, though," I murmur into his solid chest.

"Not tonight. You've got wine, and we've got the girls, but soon, Leigh, really fucking soon." It's then I take a deep breath and hold it in. Of course, my lungs fill with his scent, making my mind cloud with everything Nix.

6

NIX

"Dude, that's not where it goes," Emmy tells Rory as we're working on the first car I bought as a teenager, then worked on it night and day in what's now my shop. It was a pile of rust, filled with bondo body filler. I saved for three summers alone to pay for the car, then working and sinking another year's worth of wages to get the Camaro to where it was running solid. That didn't include the body work. Now, a shit ton of years later, it's lovingly restored, and I see the look in Rory's eyes. I love that girl like she's my own, but no fucking way would I put her behind the wheel of something that goes too damn fast only for her to wind up wrapped around a tree.

"Yes, it does, dude!" Rory responds. I'm on a crawler beneath the car, changing the fluids in the 1978 Camaro Z28 with a V8 engine. I fucking think not. Neither Rory nor Emmy will get this car. They want something old and vintage, they'll work for it. Even still, a V8 anything won't be for them.

"Dudettes, one of you gonna hand me the wrench, or do I need to do it myself?" I break through their argument. Not like either of them will put anything away correctly, which is an annoyance when I'm at the shop, but here at home, while they're with me, I give zero fucks.

"Oh crap, here you go, Nix." Emmy slides under the car beside me, not caring that she's getting dirt and oil all over her clothes. Rory, on the other hand, is busy taking pictures of herself with the Camaro in the background. Sometimes I wonder if she's not related to my sister. A girly-girl through and through, whereas Leigh has her moments when she doesn't mind getting dressed up, but she prefers to stay in sweats while curled up on the couch.

"Thanks, buttercup. You two getting your arguing out now so you won't do it to your mom tonight?" It's Saturday, a day I'd usually be at the shop, but when Leigh mentioned she was working today, I finagled a few things around so I could hang with them. It's not that the girls can't stay home alone at this age, but why should they if I can help out? Plus, it's no big deal to hang out with the two beauties who look so much like their mother it socks you in the gut, reminding me of the time when Leigh was a teenager herself.

"I suppose. It depends on Rory. Why do girls go stupid when it comes to boys and being popular? It's so dumb. I wish Fif were here," Emmy says, using my sister's nickname. A name Rory came up with when she tried to say Ophelia's name for the first time as a toddler.

"Fif was just here. Why don't you FaceTime her? You

know she'll always answer your calls." If Emmy is bringing up the boy issue, it's about time Rosaleigh has a talk with her. If not, it'll be me doing the talking with Rory, along with whatever boy she brings over.

"It's not the same. Mom is always tired, Fif is away more than she's home, and Rory's always emo over something. The only cool person lately is you." I hand Emmy the wrench, nodding at the bolt she'll need to loosen to drain the oil into the pan. I scoot out of her way, letting her do the dirty work that Rory said she wanted to. Another point in Emmy's book, the girl calling it like she is, not that I care. At least Rory still wants to hang out with me instead of with friends who are up to no good.

"I hear you, kiddo. Your mom's doing the best she can with the circumstances you three were dealt." It was hard not to notice the way Leigh was practically trying to climb her way inside me the other night, the weight of the world landing on her shoulders.

"It still sucks. I hate my dad. How could he do this to us, to just leave and not even look back?" I don't say anything, letting her get out the words she so badly needs to say to someone who is big enough to shoulder the burden. "Mom does it all. Rory tries to help, you know, but it's not the same. We can see how slim money gets, no matter how much the grands take us to help give her a reprieve. It's mom wearing the same thing, never buying anything for herself, not even the wine she loves so much, and her birthday is coming up. Do you know what she told us?"

"What's that, buttercup?" The two of us watch as the oil drains from the car into the pan, waiting for it to be done so she can put the bolt back on and get to filling it with fresh oil.

"That we're not to spend a penny of our allowance or money we got from our birthdays or Christmas on her birthday. Blasphemy." Any other kid would say bullshit; not Emmy or Rory, raised around people who cuss, yet they don't, not around adults at least.

"Shit, I guess we better tell Ya-Ya to get things ready, then. How about you and Rory come up with a few ideas on what to get her, text me the list or the links. We'll get her squared away." I've already planned a few tricks up my sleeve, including getting Ophelia to work her magic in the shopping department as well as getting her ass home. Rosaleigh and the girls have gone through a lot of firsts without Douchebag David around. Emmy's, then Rory's birthday, Thanksgiving, and Christmas. Now it's Leigh's first birthday as a single parent, and it won't be one where she's sitting at home alone after the girls have gone to bed, savoring the bottle of wine I brought over earlier this week. She thought I didn't see how she slowly took small sips, not letting me pour her more than half a glass, saying she was tired and wouldn't be able to wake up the next day if she drank too much. Little does she know it makes me want to spoil her and the girls that much more.

"You'd do that? Of course, you'd do that. I swear, Nix, you're the best." Emmy scoots closer, already preparing for what she's about to do, and kisses my cheek.

"Nah, that'd be the James girls, without a doubt. You ready to take care of the rest?" I ask as she wiggles her way out from under the car, giving me her answer that way as I use my feet to push the crawler out from under it as well.

"Duh! That's the best part, but don't tell Rory. She'll ask to do it, but she barely lifted a finger." Emmy rolls her eyes as I do an ab curl to stand up. Little shit. It wasn't her who got the oil filter, but she did do more than Rory, who is currently sitting in the driver's seat, taking selfie after selfie.

"Grab the oil. I'm gonna talk to Rory for a few minutes. You remember how much to put in?" I ask.

"Yep. You better watch out, Nix. I may take one of the boys' jobs before you know it." Emmy's not wrong. In a few years, I figure she'll be right beside me at the shop, doing tasks that my father started me out on, not caring that she's dirty or sweaty.

"Anytime you're ready." We bump knuckles as we stand up. I make my way toward Rory, who, as soon as she sees me, is putting the phone away. Son of a bitch. That's never a good sign when it comes to being a teenager. Been there, done that, and probably did way fucking worse than what she could ever imagine.

"You get the shot?" I ask, grinning at the way she blushes at getting caught.

"Yeah, sorry I didn't help any." I shrug my shoulders. This is the usual for Rory. There's a reason she wanted to hang out, and it's usually because once the car is put back together, we go for a ride, no destination in sight. The windows will be down, classic rock is always blaring, and smiles are plastered on both girls' faces.

"You okay?" I ask. Seems my girls have a shit ton on their minds lately.

"I will be. Boys are dense, you know." Figures it would be boy trouble. I arch my eyebrow at her, a sign for 'tell me something I didn't already know.'

"That's why right now, you focus on school and family. Don't fuck around with boys who are only after one or two things." I don't elaborate because she scrunches her nose up in distaste. "Exactly. Now, you wanna fire the car up when your sister's done filling up the oil?"

"Does a bear poop in the woods?"

"Say it with me, *'Does a bear shit in the woods?'*" The worry of boys is gone, and Emmy's worry will be taken care of. Right now, there's only one thing I'm going to let them worry about, and that's having fun.

7

ROSALEIGH

Thank God, I have the next two days off. Minnie was able to make it into the nursery today, took one look at me, and declared I'd have Sunday off, which we're only open a half day, but giving me Monday off as well is a total win. Chef's freaking kiss. I must look as tired as I feel for her to say that. Tomorrow, we're all going to Ya-Ya's, dinner will be covered as well as dessert, and if I even thought about bringing anything with me, she'd probably chase me around the kitchen with the closest thing possible. That means another night off this week from cooking, allowing me to save a few of my planned meals for the following week, which is better for my bank account right about now. The holidays may be over, but that doesn't mean the bills stop there, and sadly, I'm still recovering from said holidays.

I'm just stepping out of my SUV that's parked in the driveway. As much as I hate the gas guzzler, she's been good to me. I even apologized to her after cussing her out at the gas station. I've got six more months before the Tahoe will be paid off and the bank note on it will be over, allowing me to breathe easier. So, while gas is a bitch, not having a payment is smarter. I will not be trading in my old girl, no way. There's light at the end of the tunnel. That's when I hear the deep growl of Nix's Camaro round the corner. "Jesus," I breathe out, watching as he glides the car down the street with two girls inside it, one up front and one in the back. A song about giving someone a *Whole Lotta Love* is lighting up the neighborhood. I'm tired of refusing to admit he's the reason I'm able to get through my hardest days, the reason my girls have the biggest smiles plastered on their faces, the reason my knees go weak. Nix is becoming my reason for everything. I shut my car door and instead of going inside, I make my way toward the three of the most beautiful people in the world with a pep in my step, knowing that after feeling Nix pressed against me earlier this week, he clearly feels something for me, even if it's just sexual attraction. It's been so long, too long in fact, since I've felt something between my thighs besides my fingers or a vibrator. Even the battery-operated variety is hard to use—the loud buzzing could wake the girls up, or one loud moan while I'm imagining what it would be like if it were Nix using the toy on me. Even the shower is an off-limits area for me to have some peace and quiet in fear of one of the girls barging in, which happens on the regular.

"Mom! Did you hear the car? I helped with that!" Emmy is pushing Rory's seat up, folding her inside the Camaro so she can get out of the backseat. I'm wearing my standard uniform—a tee shirt with Minnie's nursery emblazoned on it, khaki shorts that hit mid thigh, and sneakers—but judging by the look on Nix's face, you'd think I weren't wearing a single stitch of clothing.

"I saw, and pray tell, what did you do to help Nix do to his Camaro? I'm pretty sure it sounded that way since I was a teenager." Emmy looks at me like I've uncovered gold. Yeah, kid, I'm old, but Nix is older, aging like fine freaking wine even if he is only a few years older than me.

"He's had the Camaro that long? Geesh, you two are older than dirt. Don't worry though, Mom, Nix, you two don't look a day over eighty." I see the grease under her eye, another smear across her jawline, proof that she did work on the car today.

"Well, isn't that the nicest compliment you ever did say." She gives me a quick kiss to the cheek as her form of saying hello.

"It was fun. Do you think I can spend the night at Katie's tonight? Now, before you say anything, I know Ya-Ya's is tomorrow, but we won't stay up too late, and I'll be ready when you come to get me, promise!" Emmy is a master negotiator, or manipulator, whichever you want to call it.

"That's fine. I have the next two days off work. Are her parents picking you up?" I ask. We've always had an agreement with most of the parents the girls hang out with—one parent drops off, the other picks up, and vice versa.

"Yep. Now, all you have to do is get rid of the older one, then you can enjoy a night of calm and tranquility." I roll my eyes at her statement.

"Go pack your bags, and be nice to your sister." She looks at me, points her finger to her chest as if saying, *Who, me?*

"Come on, Rory, don't you have plans to make, too, or boys to text? Gag me with a stick," Emmy responds about boys. I was hoping I'd have a few more years, maybe a year at best, before that started happening. The talk we had last summer obviously needs to be refreshed if boys are texting. Emmy could be exaggerating, but that doesn't seem the case when Nix gives me a look of his own, one that has him clenching his jaw. Message received, big guy.

"Hey, Nix." I walk up to him, rest my hand on his chest, going to the tips of my toes to give him a kiss on his cheek. Bold move? Probably, but neither of the girls react in a way that makes it awkward, not even when Nix wraps his hand around my hip, returning the kiss to the other side of my cheek.

"Hey, Leigh. That talk needs to happen," he whispers against the shell of my ear. The only problem is, he's been saying this for the past week, so which conversation is he referring to?

"Tonight?" I respond. Goose bumps slide down the length of my body, reaching down to the soles of my feet when I can't hold the stance of being on my toes any longer.

"That'd be a good idea." I step away. Nix lets my hip go. His heat surrounding me is now gone, leaving the ghost of a sensation in its wake.

"Rory, are you planning on living in the Camaro?" She's yet to get out of the car, whether that's to give me time to talk to Nix or if there's another reason, like being glued to her phone. I'd make more of a stink about it if she weren't so focused on school and sports Monday through Friday. On the weekends, she deserves to be a kid. Although it may come off a little selfish, teenagers have that trait engrained in them by the time they hit thirteen.

"I'm not opposed to living in it. Maybe I can become one with the car?" she replies.

"You're screwed. Do you realize what she's after?" I turn to Nix. He's already shaking his head. Thankfully, we're on the same page. Not for nothing, but he wouldn't even allow me to drive his Camaro and still has yet to this date, not that I've asked in the recent years.

"Nope, she knows it's not going to her. We had that talk before. I don't care the amount of stars in her eyes she gives me, or the pouting. It's not happening. I wouldn't be able to live with myself if, God forbid, something happened." Seriously, the only amazing thing David gave me were two girls; the man in front of me has given me so much more.

"That's a relief. I'll get her home so you can have some kind of reprieve. Thank you for taking care of them today. They love you, you know?" I place my hands in my pockets to keep them from touching him.

"The feeling is mutual. I'll come over later on. We'll have that talk, and Leigh?" He stops me from moving toward Rory to coax her out of the Camaro.

"Yes, Nix?"

"Drink your wine. You need another bottle, I'll bring it to you." Seems he's noticed more than I hoped for. His eyes land on the necklace he gave me after Emmy was born, the girls' birthstones nestled next to one another. As for the jewelry David game me, it's gone—pawned, hawked, sold, whatever you want to call it. The gold chain Nix gave me, that I will never sell or give away. Everything else, though, was fair game. His parents didn't understand it at the time, until I laid it out for them. The girls were at Nix's parents' one day when they stopped by. All of the bills were on the kitchen table. I was drowning in debt, not having moved to full-time work as of yet. That's when they got it, even attempted to help me out financially, but I refused. The only thing I'd let them help me with was clothes, school supplies, and helping me take the girls to and from when needed.

"Nix." I close my eyes. If he realizes I've cut other things out, well, that's a conversation I'd rather not have.

"Can't I stay here a smidge longer?" Rory asks, pushing as much as she can.

"Not up for discussion. Rory girl, you know I love you, but the Camaro needs to go back to the shop. I can't take you all to Ya-Ya's and Papou's in this car, so say goodbye to Black Betty." It seems Nix is helping me out yet again.

"Thanks, Nix." Rory unfolds from the car, comes over to Nix, giving him a hug, then walks to me, an arm going around my shoulder, since we're not the same height. "Madre, I'm going to see if Mary feels like company tonight."

"Anytime, Rory," Nix responds. Heat blazes in his eyes when they land on mine.

"Let me know. The sooner, the better, so I can figure out dinner, okay?" I tell her. In all honestly, it's so I can take a shower, throw on some comfy clothes, and ditch the bra.

"Later, Leigh." I nod in agreement. Even if Nix does come

over, I'll throw on a baggy shirt. I'm officially off the clock for two days, minus dinner at his parents'. Operation Dress Like a Bum is about to commence.

8

NIX

After the girls and Leigh left, it was time for me to work around the inside and outside of the house, knowing tomorrow was going to be one where I'd be surrounded by the best of both worlds. What the girls don't know is that I've got a trick up my sleeve, one that I think all of them could use right about now. So, I got to work. Since I was already dirty, I started with the yard work, taking my shirt off, pulling the lawn mower out, and getting shit done. By the time I had sweat dripping off my body, I noticed Rosaleigh was sitting on her front porch, changed from her work clothes into a tank top and cut-off jean shorts. I was tempted to quit what I was doing, to walk over to her house and have that talk we've been needing to have, and I probably would if the girls still weren't home. Instead, I just kept trucking along, mowing, then pulling out the weed eater to finish the job, stealing glances at the beauty who had no problem keeping her eyes locked on me. Believe me, it wasn't an easy task, especially when I caught her out of the corner of my eye, gaze lingering on my body while her teeth were pressing into her lower lip.

I waited this long. A few more hours weren't going to hurt me. So, I did what I needed on the outside of the house until the yard was back in shape. In a couple more weeks, I'd have to deal with it again. I've been a bachelor all of my thirty-three years. I'm that schmuck who wanted the girl he thought he never could have. Now it seems like all the waiting was worth it. Not being able to touch Leigh like I wanted once Douchebag David cut and run, knowing the pain she and the girls would be going through, it was hard. Especially when Rory and Emmy had no problem running to me when it was a shoulder they needed to lean on or an ear to listen to their worries. The only person who was reluctant in doing so was Leigh.

"Fuck," I grumble into the tiled shower, my hand ready to jack my cock, remembering how Rosaleigh felt pressed up against me when I caught her sneaking into her own house, knowing that the blush that creeped along her chest onto her neck was because of me, nipples hard and pebbled, ready to be sucked on by me and me alone. I turn the water from hot to cold, refusing to cum in my hand again. The next time it happens, it's going to be my cum painting Leigh's pretty little body or fucking it into her cunt. That image does nothing to calm my aching dick down. Who the fuck am I fooling? There's nothing that doesn't make me hard when it comes to the woman across the street. I turn off the water and step out of the shower soaking wet, hoping now that I'm dripping wet from the cold water. Maybe the cool air in the house will make my cock calm the hell down. I grab the towel, drying myself off while I stand on the carpeted rug.

There was once a time I thought about walking away from everything, cutting my losses, and starting a life where I didn't have to watch the woman I knew was meant to be mine give her love to a piss-poor fucker, only for him to turn into the worst kind of human he could ever become. I shake the thoughts out of my head. Tonight, I'm going to stake my claim. I'm going to make her mine.

"Yo," I answer the phone when it starts vibrating on the counter in the bathroom, seeing it's Ophelia who's calling me.

"Ugh, you're such a Neanderthal. Who answers the phone with *Yo?*"

"And who answer the phone with *Ugh?* This isn't the days of *Clueless. As if* isn't appropriate either, little sister." It's nothing for us to volley back insults to one another; that's what siblings are for.

"Anyways, I was calling because I've got my ticket booked for Leigh-Leigh's birthday. Then I got a call an hour ago from my Rory baby, then Emmy Lou back-to-back. What the fuck is going on? Both of the girls in one day? This has my big brother written all over it. What gives?" I can hear the city noise in the background. Whereas I wanted stay in Abalee, take over the auto shop, and set down roots, Ophelia had other plans, moving to the city in another state, kicking ass in her career of choice, working with high-profile clients when it comes to million-dollar looks as a fashion stylist.

"Girls are having a rough go of things. Rory misses you, and Emmy is pissed that Leigh doesn't want them to do anything for her birthday. Though I think that's because money is tight, and you know your best friend. She won't take handouts even if I make it seem like a loan. The only thing I can do is make them dinner, buy her some wine, and watch her suffer in silence." I run a hand through my hair, having wrapped the towel around me before answering the call. If anyone knows Leigh more than me, it's Ophelia. The only problem being is she's in Hollywood currently, working on some movie, which means my sister isn't here to help out when needed, like today. When both girls dropped the proverbial plate on my lap.

"Cheese and rice, I could tell something was bugging them, but both said they were going to a friend's house tonight. Which means Leigh-Leigh is going to be home alone." Ophelia isn't an idiot. My intentions once Douchebag David was out of the picture wasn't hard to notice.

"Yep, I know. You think it's finally hitting the girls about what their father did is still carrying over all these months later?" I ask her, ignoring the fact that both girls will be gone for the night. Emmy came out and said it; Rory alluded to doing something similar. Looks like luck is on my side. Leigh and I will get that talk I've been wanting to have.

"Probably. The girls have all kinds of hormonal changes going on. They're watching their mother do it all. Not that Leigh-Leigh wasn't before. That dumb fuck. She never could see that she was a single mom while married. He'd say he was working an extra shift. If that were the case, he wouldn't have had to get in bed with a cartel, and where did all the money go from all of this shit anyways? Because, as far as I can tell, Leigh-Leigh isn't rolling in the green." Ophelia is fired up, more pissed than Rosaleigh was when everything came out. I'm pretty sure she took a red-eye home after I made the call, kicking and screaming, ready to kick Douchebag David's ass. Ophelia would have to get in line because I'm gonna kick it first if he ever shows himself again.

"You're preaching to the choir, Fif." I use the kids' name for her, trying to calm her down. One thing about Ophelia— if you fuck around, you're gonna find out. My sister might come in a tiny package, but her bite is bigger than her bark.

"So, since the girls are going to be gone, are you making your move, big brother?" I walk out of the bathroom, seeing the laundry piled up in my room, knowing that I've got a few more things to take care of before I even think about crossing the street.

"Something like that. The sooner this conversation is over, the faster I can get shit done. Head to the store to pick her up another bottle of wine and something to eat, seeing as Emmy purged on me today saying Leigh wasn't drinking the last bottle but savoring it." I don't go into the fact that most of the clothes she wears have been washed a hundred times over, even with Ophelia dumping piles of clothes on all three of them when she comes home. I know Leigh; she's putting them away for Rory and Emmy, leaving nothing for herself once again.

"Go get her, tiger. The next time I'm in town, I'll ply her with the good stuff. She usually opens up after that. Last time, it was hard with the family competing for everyone's attention." Ophelia doesn't admit it was because she was only home for three days before there was some catastrophe causing her to leave shortly after we all opened presents together.

"Later, Fif. Love you, girl."

"Love you. Go get your woman." We hang up. I grab a pair of clean boxer briefs, sliding them up my legs, then do the same with a pair of jeans. After I'm dressed, it's time to tackle the pile of laundry that's creating a mountain in my bedroom, along with the dishes in the sink. Fuck, I've let shit pile up this week. At least it was for a good cause. Spending time with Leigh and her daughters, it's all fucking worth it.

9

ROSALEIGH

A rare night off, that's what I'm going to have. A night where I don't have to stress about the girls needing to go here or having to be picked up at some weird-ass time when the movies let out. Which usually means I can't shower or take my bra off because my car is piled with extra kids. Believe me, I try not to complain too much. I was their age once, had a shit home life, did everything in my power to stay out of my mom and her flavor of the month's way. At least the girls don't have it that bad. I'm not downplaying their situation; their father gave them a shit hand. The upside is, I knew from a very early age the moment I became a mom, my kids would be my world. There wasn't one golden or magical cock that would make me choose a guy over my kids. I'd never become my mother, that's for sure.

It's me, the couch, clothes that don't require a bra or panties, and the television on some kind of cooking show that I'm not really listening to, using it more for background noise than anything else. A glass of wine in my hand, head tipped to the ceiling, and enjoying a rare moment to myself. One where I'm not in the car thinking about everything I have to do once I get home, or late at night when I'm trying to sleep but there's always a constant worry. Is the laundry done, are the girls really okay with how things are right now, can they hear me in the dead of night when the only thing that puts me to sleep is Nix. Let me rephrase that—it's the fantasies of the tall, dark, and handsome man. You know, the one who rescues me time and time again, even if it's from myself. That last time, my body molding to his, trying to sink further into Nix, the length of his cock showing me how big he is, and I've got to tell you, that night definitely went into my spank bank material.

My body shivers as I take a sip of my wine, replaying how my imagination ran wild later that night, about him sneaking into my room, dropping his clothes as I came awake feeling his presence like I always do when Nix is near, ripping the covers from my body, doing the same to my clothes until we were skin to skin, his length hot and heavy between my spread thighs, my hips cradling his body, finally getting to feel his lips against mine, his big hands, work-roughened from his years of using them on repairing cars and trucks as they skate along my body. My eyes close and my head tips back, using the glass to calm down the beating of my heart to cool me off.

"Leigh, I know you're in there. Unlock the door, woman. My hands are full." He scares the shit out of me, so much so that I almost drop my wine.

"I'm coming, I'm coming!" I place my wine on the coffee table, stand up, and make my way to the door, all while grumbling under my breath, "You almost were. A few more minutes, and you'd be screaming Nix's name. That could have been awkward."

"Finally. You know, I've been knocking on the door a few minutes now. I almost used the code to open the door." That's how Nix greets me when I open the door, feeling the cool breeze from the night air as he dips his head down, lips going to the underside of my jaw, placing a kiss there, stealing the words from my mouth. A kiss on the cheek or a hug, is usually all he gives me, until recently, and while a part of my brain wants to say, 'Abort mission. All men are bad, have ulterior motives, and will break your heart,' when it comes to Phoenix Drakos, I know that's absolutely not the case. He's the best kind of man who could ever be. How he's managed to stay single all this time, I'm not sure because he's one of a kind.

"What did you buy this time?" I ask, closing the door, realizing that the cool air also brought in another problem. My arm bands around my chest as I look for a jacket. Usually, between three girls, there're clothes strewn around the house everywhere. That's not the case here tonight. Not a shirt, jacket, or robe is in sight. The only person to blame is myself, too. After the girls went to their friend's house, I decided it would be a grand idea to dust, vacuum, and pick up everything and anything that wasn't in its place. Good job, Rosaleigh.

"Wine, bourbon, some charcuterie thing that was already done. A few things the girls mentioned you cut back on for yourself. We're gonna have words about that, too." I follow him inside the house after I shut the door, hearing the lock engage. Great, that's just what I need. I love my girls, and I know they're doing their best to help me, but damn, some things they could at least pretend to keep to themselves.

"Something tells me this conversation is going to require more listening and not a whole lot of talking on my part." My eyes pop out of my head, I'm sure of it, jaw dropping as well as I watch Nix take out the groceries from the plethora of bags he carried in. There's his bottle of bourbon he prefers, Makers Mark, and not one, not two, but three bottles of the Pinot Noir I prefer. The same brand he brought the other day. It's not expensive, but it sure as hell isn't cheap. Three of those bottles is half of my grocery budget a week. When there were two incomes, it was nothing to add a bottle once a week, or once every other week, to the mix. Things have changed. Accounts were seized that I didn't even know about. Even our joint checking account was until some kind of forensic something or other to make sure it was only David's check being deposited and not stolen money.

"I want you as a willing participant. Pretty sure I'm going to need your pretty voice in order for that to happen." Nix pulls out the charcuterie tray as well, which is basically a fruit, cheese, and meat tray that is in danger of overflowing. That also comes with a hefty price tag that you could make at home for half the price. I know because the girls and I did it one day when they were tired of sandwiches for dinner after I closed at the nursery.

"You do realize it would have been cheaper if we cooked instead of getting that?" My arm is still wrapped around my chest. That way, I don't flash Nix with my high beams. The need for a jacket is still at the forefront of my mind. "I'll be right back. I need to go grab something from my room."

"That may be, but a night off doesn't consist of cooking or cleaning. Don't feel like you have to cover up on my account, Leigh. I felt your body against mine. Know what I do to you. There's no pretenses with how I want you. Waited a fuck of a long time, and I'll wait even longer. What I don't want you to do is hide from me, not your feelings, and definitely not your body." Well, you can't say Nix never states what he's thinking, at least not tonight. That's probably why, instead of going to my bedroom to grab a hoodie or to change completely, I do the complete opposite. I drop my arm and close the distance between the two of us, skirting around the peninsula until I'm standing in front of him.

"I'd rather you show me than tell me." The words that come out of my mouth are not the wife of a man she lost her virginity to, a now single mother doing everything on her own, leaving little to no time for herself. Tonight, though, I'm being Rosaleigh, a woman who wants the man in front of her more, to feel the sensation that only Nix elicits. And when he groans deep in his chest, head dipping down, I know I'm about to experience a moment with Phoenix Drakos that I've been dreaming about for what seems like eternity.

10

NIX

"Fuck it," I mutter. I dip my head, lips grazing the softest set of lips I could ever dream of, finally feeling them, tongue snaking out to lick at the plushness. Taste the sweet undercurrents of the crisp wine she's been drinking. I'm only hoping she's not going to regret this once it's over. My hand moves to her hip, knowing that with one movement, the palm of my hand could have her lush skin beneath it. Leigh was worth the wait, worth the turmoil of watching her fall for the wrong guy, even if that guy was once my best friend. I watched the way he manipulated the situation, biding my time even when it put me in the permanent friend zone, a place I never wanted to be. I pull Leigh's body closer to mine, wishing she were sitting on a barstool, wanting her to cushion my body as I deepen the kiss.

"Nix." The soft purr that carries from the back of her throat into mine... Son of a bitch. Too long, too fucking long

I've waited for Rosaleigh not to be David's anymore, to be right where I am. I work it so she can't back away. My hand delves into the loose strands at the base of her neck, combing through the blonde locks, holding her mouth captive to mine as my tongue sweeps inside. Her hands that were by her sides move until they're gliding from where they were, pressing against my lower abdomen. I'm worried she's going to push me away, but she does the exact opposite as her fingers clench in the fabric of my black cotton shirt, pulling me closer.

"Jesus, your mouth, sweetheart." I pull away for a moment, eyes opening, watching what our kiss does to her. The proof is right before me. Rosaleigh has her eyes closed, and she's breathing heavy much like myself, and the once creamy skin now has a red hue to it.

"You're one to talk." She takes a moment to respond. I'm unsure if that's a good or a bad thing. There's a part of me that wants to say fuck it, to take Leigh to bed, not worrying about talking or where her head is at. I won't. There's too much left unsaid, and there's a a deep-seated need for Leigh to know she won't regret this come tomorrow morning.

"Temptation, that's what you are, Rosaleigh, and as enticing as it is to keep going, I'm thinking we need to clear the air." I massage the base of her neck. Leigh's head tips backwards, a moan slides out, and shit, that is not doing anything for my aching cock. At the rate we've been going, I'm going to have a calloused palm as well as a permanent zipper imprint on my damn cock.

"So you've said a few times about this communication thing." She is still locked between my body and the counter, neither of us willing to move just yet. I watch as she takes another deep breath, trying to slow down her rapidly beating heart as my thumb slides along her pulse while my other fingers work at the tension that is slowly leaving her neck.

"Yep. You mind pouring the drinks? I'll grab the tray of food and get the fire pit started so you're not freezing." Our eyes are locked. I'm not willing to move an inch just yet, and she seems to be content just the same.

"I don't mind at all. I need to grab my phone, too, in case one of the girls calls. Not that I really expect them to." She shrugs her shoulders. There goes that weight of the world again, settling in. Rory and Emmy I get. What a woman like Rosaleigh shouldn't have to worry about is the incessant worry about working, making enough money to pay the bills, and how she's going to juggle being a mom at the same time.

"You know as well as I do, they'll be texting you at some point, even if it's to say good night. Grab your phone, and a blanket for you, too. I'll meet you out back." My lips seek hers, wanting another taste for pure selfish reasons. A niggle of fear is working its way into my system that Leigh may not want to start anything after the turmoil she's been through.

"Thanks." Right now, there doesn't seem to be a worry. The way she had no problem responding to my kiss, I'd say we're on even playing level. I step back, allowing her to get the drinks ready as I fish out the charcuterie whatever board and pull the wrapper off it. I didn't give a fuck the cost if it meant we could both enjoy an evening away from other shit besides what's working between us right now.

"No problem, sweetheart." My eyes laser in on her backside as she turns around. Rosaleigh may have lost more weight than she should have, but that doesn't mean she lost all of her curves. She's got strong shoulders, a lean waist, hips that flare out, and an ass to make a man weak, paired with the cotton shorts she's wearing, showing off her lean legs. A tank top that should be illegal in all fifty states. My mouth waters at the thought of sliding the fabric off her body, desperately seeking what she would look like when my lips attached to her pebbled nipples. Yeah, Douchebag David is definitely a fucking idiot, and given the chance, I'd work my ass off to make her forget about the man who ripped her world apart, abandoning her and their two amazing little girls. Girls who, given the chance, I'd take as my own even though my blood isn't flowing through their veins.

It doesn't take me long to grab the platter and unlock the back door, another battle that I see is now being implemented after I replaced this lock as well. That one is on me. The first thing I should have done when Douchebag David walked out was change or re-key everything. Sadly, it was the last thing on my mind when the three little women were struggling the most. I made my presence known then and let things fall by the wayside. I put the platter on the outdoor loveseat Leigh has set up, two chairs on either side, cushioned, well-loved and well used, yet still holding on strong. She has a way of making things work in her favor, is not above hitting up a thrift store or a garage sale, bringing it home, having her girls load and off-load it if I'm not around. Then she re-imagines shit I could never even fathom, sanding this, cutting that, painting a piece of furniture if she can't get it to her liking. Some might think it looks tacky, but when it's all said and done, you would never know that she picked up the two patio end tables for five bucks.

I move off the wooden deck and walk around the side of the deck to flip the switch for the outdoor fire pit Rosaleigh picked up a few months ago, another one of her finds, practically brand new. She grabbed it for a steal at the local thrift store because a contractor couldn't use it. Of course, that meant me spending a Saturday over here and running a gas line. The company, the food, and the view were worth it. Which reminds me, I bet Leigh hasn't checked her gas tank, seeing as how I've yet to see or hear her complain about the hefty bill that comes with having it refilled.

"Nix, what are you working on now?" Rosaleigh says as I flip the switch. I won't have time to take a look at the gas levels now. If she knows what I'm up to, it'll be another worry that I don't want her thinking about tonight.

"I'm not. Just walked down here to flip the switch. The idiot who installed the line could have made it easier for you to get to." I clearly wasn't thinking it would be smarter to have it on a switch near the patio wall instead of near the main shut-off to the propane.

"It's not that difficult to walk down a few stairs. My feet aren't that delicate." I walk back up the steps, one hand on the railing. The flicker from the fire illuminates her beauty. She's got both hands full with our drinks, a blanket draped over her forearm. And thank you, God, she didn't cover up a stitch of her body.

I arch my eyebrows at her statement. The woman doesn't

mind working with her hands, but I know for a fact that she does not like her feet dirty, so it surprises me that she's on the back porch barefoot. "Okay, fine. I can wear shoes, you know. Besides, I like it back there. I won't have to worry about one of the girls or their friends accidentally flipping the switch and a catastrophe happening."

"Fine, I'll leave it be. You ready to eat and have a drink?" I ask her as I walk closer, my hand going to the one that's holding my bourbon neat without ice like I prefer.

"Yeah, maybe I should have brought our bottles out as well."

"I'll grab them if we need them." I clasp her glass as well as she takes a seat and watch as she curls her legs beneath her ass, placing the blanket across her lap, leaving the top part of her body in just a tank. Lucky fucking me. "Food first, then we'll talk. One of the subjects is going to make me more uncomfortable than you. Can't believe Rory is thirteen, boys are fucking sniffing around, and shit if it doesn't worry me to no end." I sit down beside her, grab the platter so it's within reaching distance for the two of us.

"I know. God, I know. We've had the talk multiple times, and I know a more serious one is going to have to happen, or she's going to have a flip phone." I listen to Leigh as I take a healthy sip of my bourbon, letting the burn slide down my throat.

"Thank fuck. Emmy brought up that Rory is always on her phone, some boy has her attention, and how she thinks it's stupid. Emmy doesn't realize she'll be there soon. That's gonna keep me up all night when there're boys sniffing around both girls." I'm not exaggerating either.

"Shit, can you imagine the boy who tries to tame Emmy? I feel sorry for the fool already. Rory, on the other hand, I see so much of myself in her. I just hope she doesn't follow in my footsteps. She has dreams and goals. Not that I regret having my babies, but at the age I was, it wasn't easy." She is thinking about the past, which is a road I'm not going to go down. What I'm after is the future, one that has me standing beside her from now until fucking forever.

11

NIX

"We'll get the girls through this phase and come out on the other side," I say to Rosaleigh, watching as she stretches her legs. I capture her long shapely calves with one hand and pull them on my lap, setting my drink on the end table and placing the platter on her lap. Truth be told, I bought the food for her. I already ate after I worked on the inside and outside of my house, knowing this would be an indulgence much like the wine she's currently sipping, not being as cautious as she was earlier this week.

"Come hell or high water. Clearly, I thought I was doing an okay job, keeping her busy with school and sports. If Emmy is noticing a change, then it's time for me to step in." I move both of my hands beneath her blanket. Leigh hisses out a breath at my cold hands touching her warm skin. "Nix, that's not very nice. Your hands are like icicles." She goes to move her legs off where I placed them on my lap, but I hold strong.

"That's why I need you to warm me up, sweetheart." I use both hands massaging one calf. Leigh no longer complains about my freezing hands that are now warm from her skin. I keep myself still, not pushing it when what I'd really like to do is work my way up her body to feel her muscles tense beneath the palms of my hands as I knead each delicious inch until she spreads her thighs open for me, unknowing if it'd be my mouth or my hands on her pussy first.

"Don't stop." Her eyes close, wine glass resting against her neck.

"I'm not, not now and not fucking ever. I'm telling you right now, Rosaleigh. You, Rory, and Emmy, you're mine. I've been waiting, biding my time to make sure the timing was right, allowing you the time to get back on your feet, to stand on your own. It's been nearly a year. I've watched you struggle, get knocked down only to get back up. You're doing incredible." Her eyes open. I position myself so my back is to the armrest of the couch, much like she is now. It also opens her legs further, one dropping to the floor while the other is pressed against the back of the cushions.

"Phoenix Drakos, do you have any idea what you're asking for? One teenager who's testing her limits, a preteen who's full of drama, and me. Gosh, I come with a pile of baggage, so much so that it might very well break my back. Let alone yours if you take us on." If Leigh is trying to talk me out of making her mine, of making her girls mine, she's got another thing coming. All I can see from the time I wake up until the time I go to sleep is these three women. Some nights, they follow me in my dreams, giving me something I could only hope and dream for—my family.

"Sweetheart, you let me worry about the weight. That kiss you gave me in the kitchen sealed the deal. Add the way you haven't been pulling away any time I get my hands on you, it means you're mine and I'm yours. Rory and Emmy help complete the circle." I move my hands up higher, watching as she places the food and her glass of wine on the table by her head, body twisting as she moves. The fabric of her top lifts, giving me a view of her stomach, and when she has to really arch her body, the underside of her breasts are right there. I lick my lips, watching as she moves back to where she was, her pebbled nipples only getting harder as my hands keep working the muscles of her outer thighs, thumbs dragging across the inside, getting dangerously close to where I want to lick, taste, and feel.

"I'm dreaming, aren't I? Right, this is a dream. You're offering this on a silver platter. Maybe I shouldn't have put my wine down after all." Unable to stand another moment of Leigh putting any kind of self-doubt between the two of us, I make my move, cussing the small couch, when what we both could use is a bed beneath our bodies. What I don't miss is the rapid rising and falling of her chest or the way her eyes heat with unhidden desire.

"It's not a dream. It's reality, a reality I'm going to make sure you're a part of every step of the way." I pause, letting Rosaleigh see the truth in my words, knowing I'll bust my ass to make any reservation she has about us starting a relationship go away.

"Nix, I'm not even divorced from David yet. Which I'm

realizing now should have happened after the news was delivered and there was a smear campaign against me by the media. Thank God our town didn't show me their backs. That would have sucked. Oh, that reminds me. Do you know of a good divorce attorney?" I wasn't expecting to bring up this conversation while my cock is hard as a rock while sitting across from Rosaleigh in clothes that leave little to the imagination. Lucky me on that front, but I could do without Douchebag David.

"Leigh, you didn't see it because you were blind to any and all things David. The town loves you. Him, not so much. We'll talk about that later, though. Thinking that might be a mood killer. And while I'm not interested in only taking you to bed, I doubt very seriously you want to delve into the past." She gives me that soft look of hers, one she reserves for the girls when they're talking about mundane things like their day at school, who's failing what or who's dating whom. I get that, for the first time in all my time of knowing Rosaleigh, she's giving me something more than I could ever ask for. "As for the divorce attorney, I can ask Eli at work who he used." I move her body until she's straddling my lap.

"Oh, well, yes, if you could ask Eli. From what I read online, since he's a wanted fugitive, we'll just have to put a notice in the newspaper, and if he doesn't respond, voilà!" The blanket drops to the side, and a shiver works through her body.

"Good. You need help, don't hesitate to ask. We'll call it an early birthday present for myself." She throws her head back, arms looping around my neck, and let's go, wild and free.

"As funny as that is, you can pay for the celebratory drinks. There's a reason I've been nickeling and diming myself to death. I've got five thousand saved for the attorney. I wasn't sure what the cost would be if this gets dragged out." Goose bumps appear on her skin as my hands slide beneath her shirt, feeling her skin once again. When she moves her body closer, I know she feels what having her on my lap and in my hands does to me.

"That mean we're on the same page? Because I've gotta tell you, Leigh, I'm not taking no for an answer, and I'm not giving up either." If I have to play dirty, bend her to my will with my mouth, fingers, and cock, that's what I'll do. "I know you want this. I get that you're apprehensive. That's why I'm going to promise you something first. No sex, not yet. I'm not putting a timestamp on it. It'll happen when you're ready and you feel secure that this relationship is real and lasting."

"You're really going to deny us both orgasms?" She is seriously asking me that question with her cotton-covered pussy pressed against my cock that I could have whipped out in less than ten seconds with a pull on the buttons.

"Not that I want to, especially when you're on top of me, all this smooth skin for the taking, knowing you've got nothing on underneath your top. And I'm willing to bet if my fingers dipped beneath the waist band of your shorts, I'd find nothing but skin. There's a reason why I'm saying no sex, no foreplay, we keep our hands to ourselves. This isn't just sex, and it's not to pass the time. When I said you and the girls were mine, I meant it, Leigh."

"Yes, we're on the same page, and while I appreciate you being a gentleman, please know in advance I'm going to do everything in my power to break your rules." Her head dips. I know what she's after, and I'm going to give her what she needs.

"You do that, I'll enjoy it every step of the way." Our lips meet, and my hand slides up the base of her spine, moving beneath the shirt. Just because I said no orgasms or sex of any kind, that doesn't mean I won't enjoy teasing Rosaleigh every step of the way.

12

ROSALEIGH

"Hmmm." I wake up, warmer than normal. Cozier, too. My eyes refuse to open after the amount of wine I consumed along with the lack of eating earlier in the day even though Nix plied me with food that was up my alley. That didn't mean it hit my system before the alcohol did, not that I'm complaining. The talk Nix and I had last night is enough to make me squeal like a teenage girl. While my marriage was a happy one, there was never the passion or excitement that exudes when I'm with Nix. It could be because David and I started young, or it could be that we were both too tired for the intimate side of things. One thing is for sure—the passion Nix gives me, the unadulterated lust, it's more than I've ever felt before.

"Go back to sleep. It's early still," the man of the hour grumbles beneath me, his vibrating chest teasing my body in more ways than one. I had no intention of getting up to begin with, not with Nix cushioning my body without a shirt. I'm in my summer pajamas in the tail end of winter. In Georgia, the weather swings wide and far—sometimes it's freeze-your-tits-off cold, other days it's hotter than Satan's butthole.

"I'm not getting up. My eyes refuse to open, and my body is telling me to stay right here." I move my body, trying to sink further into Nix's embrace, an impossible feat. My brain isn't computing the word *impossible* this morning. I'm spinning all the memories that were made last night, each of us wanting the same thing, neither of us scared to go after it, the way Nix had no problem not getting me off but made a show of how hard he was. Yep, it's clear to me that wet panties will be a thing for the foreseeable future.

"I can hear you thinking. If you're not going to go back to sleep, you may as well tip your head and give me a good-morning kiss." Another new trait I've seen from Phoenix. Where he was always in charge before, now it's like a switch has been flipped. The alpha, dominant man has come out, and there's no caging him.

"Is that a question or a demand?" My body has a mind of its own, using my toes against his pants leg to push me up further until my lips are at the column of his throat. Nix's five-o'clock shadow is more like a full day of growth, and feeling that against my lips has me imagining what he'd feel like with his head buried between my spread thighs. His hand pulls at my hair, tipping me back from where I was kissing him, lips landing on mine. Morning breath doesn't enter his mind, causing me to forget about it as well. He takes my mouth. It's not sweet and gentle. He's staking a claim, one that isn't visible for anyone else to see but enough for me to feel. I moan when he nips at my lower lip, needing and wanting more. My body moves of its own accord until I'm completely on top of him, his hands fisted in my hair, manipulating my mouth with his. My legs wrap around his hips, feeling his length, hot, hard, and heavy, body moving, craving this man beneath my body as he fucks my mouth the way a man would fuck a woman.

"Nix, more, please." I'm not above begging, trying to get him to break his promise. I rock my hips. The grip he has on my hair tightens, causing my body to tighten as well. My core spasms, grasping on to nothing.

"Not happening. You heard me loud and clear last night. I'm not taking you until you know without a shadow of a doubt that this is the real deal. That means us moving in together, me adopting the girls if that's what they want, a ring on your finger, and I know that you may not want another child, but if you're willing to do that, I'd gladly be by your side every step of the way." Nix lays it out. My raging hormones only go even more berserk.

"Jesus, Nix," I moan, still using his body as my personal playground. I'm so unbelievably close, my eyes start to close, head attempting to tip back even with the hold he has on my hair, thighs clenching, and then my orgasm that was so close is taken away. "No, no, no," I berate as Nix is off the couch and I'm standing on my feet, his hands holding my hips to steady me. The need to face plant, kick my feet back and forth while screaming into a pillow sounds like the perfect thing to do right about now. "It's been over year. Hell, it could be two years by now. I've gotten myself off more times than I care to admit to the wild fantasies running through my mind when it comes to the two of us." I attempt to pull away, ready to take care of myself. Nix does what I least expect him to, body dipping until his shoulder meets my stomach, and I'm being carried in a fireman's hold.

"I'm not making you come. You want to do that, I'll be your willing observer while you fuck that pretty pussy of yours with the toys you keep in the nightstand drawer." My hands grip his ass for purchase. I was going to try and slide down his body, stomp myself to my bedroom, slam the door, and using my shower to get off.

"How do you know about my toys?" I should be appalled about how Nix could possibly know where and if I use my battery-operated friends.

"Leigh, if you don't want me to find out that you prefer the purple vibrator with dual heads, you may want to put things back where they're hidden." I don't leave them out. My bedroom and bathroom aren't off limits when the girls are home.

"Fuck, please tell me you put them away, so the girls aren't scarred for life." I'm thinking about how I was in a rush one morning, when we all overslept. The reason for that is the man who's currently carrying me toward my bedroom. Three times I got myself off that night, yet it still didn't take the edge off, which kept me tossing and turning.

"Yeah, sweetheart, I did. That also meant I got a sneak peek of what you're using. I'm going to use that toy on you, not my fingers or my mouth, but it'll be the hottest thing I've ever witnessed watching your pussy milk the silicone cock, wishing it were mine." I don't say another word. I'm too busy having a mini orgasm from his words alone. Maybe Phoenix's rules aren't so bad after all. Plus, doesn't the saying go 'Some rules are meant to be broken'?

13

NIX

This woman is going to be the death of me, making me bend to her will, especially after she admitted how long it had been for her. Fuck, knowing that the minute I slide inside her, she'll be so tight it'll probably have me coming on the spot, if that doesn't happen this morning while she uses her favorite vibrator. It doesn't take long to make the short trip to her bedroom. Leigh put her own personal touches on her home, repurposing some of the furniture she had to revive it. The once dark house with darker furniture is gone; in its place are lighter walls, and the same goes for the décor. The best part is the new bed Leigh had me pick up with my truck one day after work. A queen-size bed, wrought iron in design, and perfect if you want to tie your woman to the wide slats, holding her in place while you take your time with her. I didn't question what reason she had to get rid of the one she and Douchebag David shared; it wasn't my place to ask, and the truth of the matter is, I was fucking ecstatic Leigh was removing Douchebag David's existence, minus what the girls wanted to remain. For the most part, though, it was pictures and a few mementos that are now stored in their rooms.

"Look at you. Fuck, but you're the most beautiful woman I've ever laid eyes on," I tell her as her back meets the mattress. Her legs squeeze together, body arching, thrusting her tits up toward me. I'm at a loss on where to start first, to stand here and stare at every delicious inch of her, to strip her out of her clothes, to strip myself out of my own so I can jack my cock while she fucks a piece of silicon in and out of her cunt, or to let go of my place on her thighs that are currently spread open. The fantasy of having Leigh like this is nothing compared to seeing it real life, her heated gaze searing my own, skin a blush color from her desire. The scent that is all Leigh permeates the air, making me want to dive headfirst, fuck the rules I laid out and get my first taste of Rosaleigh.

"Nix." My name is said in a breathless tone, and I know what I'm doing first. I step back, not leaving the room, taking my own breath even though she lets out a groan, annoyed that my hands aren't on her skin.

"Not going anywhere, sweetheart. You want the purple one or the turquoise?" I ask. She's got a few others, but they're on the smaller side. I lick my lower lip, my cock twitching beneath my jeans. What I don't expect is for Leigh to sit up, hands going to the bottom of her shirt, pulling it up and over her head.

"Purple. I don't know if I should be worried or impressed that you know which toys I have," she says as I open the drawer, one eye on Leigh, the other on what I'm going after. Tits that will fit perfectly in my hands, cherry-colored nipples that tip upwards. My mouth is dying to get a taste of them. Maybe this wasn't a good idea, especially as she drops to one hip, her bottom lip captured between her teeth. I grab the vibrator, barely able to control myself as she wiggles out of the shorts that are as tantalizing as the top.

"Impressed, especially when you're using them in front of me, watching as I work my cock so we can both come at the same time." Rosaleigh slides up on the bed, pillows at her back, completely fucking bare, no hesitation as she spreads her thighs open, giving me the prettiest sight before my eyes. "Jesus, I can't wait to get my mouth your cunt." I turn the vibrator on the lowest setting, not willing to let her use it on her own just yet. A glutton for punishment is what I am today.

"You could do that today. Foreplay isn't technically sex, right?" She tempts me. I slide the tip of the toy along one nipple. A gasp leaves her, head tipping back as I hover above her. Those delicate fingertips of Rosaleigh's are at my hips, teasing my lower abdomen in an attempt to get in my pants.

"Rosaleigh," I growl, moving the vibrator to her other nipple while I climb between her spread legs, the top of my thighs opening her further. It's a damn good thing my jeans are still on, buttons in place, because I'd probably give in right about now. "You want this inside your pussy, or do you want to use your fingers?"

"Inside me, but I want you to use it on me, or is that breaking the rules?" A question for a question. Her fingers that were only playing at my jeans manage to pop open the first button. I don't stop her. If this is what she needs, my cock is all too fucking willing.

"You want me to fuck you with this while I use my hand? I'm pretty sure this is all kinds of foreplay, Leigh. You're tempting the beast. The only way you're going to get more is once you know that this is going to happen, for-fucking-ever. If you're prepared for that, I'll do exactly as you're asking. If not, your hands stay on you and my hands stay on me." I move the toy down the center of her chest, watching as her stomach caves inward. Her eyes close. I keep the toy hovering until she gives me the answer.

"That's not fair, Nix. We have so much to talk about, and it's not like that can happen right now. Plus, the girls, they deserve to know what the two people they love in their life need to be okay, too." That's hard to compete with. It's also the answer to my question. I didn't expect this to be easy. Leigh's been hurt; she's still dealing with the after effect of a public catastrophe.

"And we'll be talking about anything and everything. There'll be no secrets, no what-ifs, no second-guessing how we feel for one another. Next time we do this, it'll be me using it on you. Today, it's going to have to be all you, sweetheart." I hit a different setting, making the vibrator hum higher and faster, then place the tip at the entrance of her pussy, going against what I said all along.

"Phoenix." Never thought I'd hear her say my name while the two of us were in bed together. Another fantasy coming to life.

"Buying a massive mirror for the next time, too, watching the lips of your cunt suck greedily at the head of this toy. It's hot as fuck." Leigh is able to open another button of my pants. My cock makes its appearance known, the sweeping of her finger gliding across it only for her to take it away just as quickly. Would have my knees buckling if I weren't sitting down. It's what she does next that has me pushing this further than I was willing to. "Son of a bitch, you're not playing fair." The pre-cum she gathered from my tip is on her thumb, and when she brings it to her mouth, that's also when I sink the toy inside her pussy, fighting fire with fire. She's wet, so wet that there's no need at all for the lube in the nightstand drawer.

"Oh God, right there," she moans as I hold the toy completely inside her, the rabbit working her clit. My other hand rips the rest of the buttons down on my jeans. Her eyes stay on mine as my fist encompasses my length.

"Take over, Rosaleigh. Show me how you use this toy as you think about me taking you, owning your pleasure as you moan my name." She wraps her hand around mine that's holding the base of her toy, not letting me go, and fuck if I want to anyways. Leigh is breaking down every barrier I could ever put up. She's an addiction, deep in my veins, a habit I never want to kick. My eyes lock on her face before they move to her tits, watching as they bounce, down to where our hands are working the purple silicon, watching as her greedy pussy grabs ahold of the toy, not letting go. It's enough to make me come right then and there, knowing that one day soon, it's going to be my cock.

"Oh God, I'm close. Come with me, Nix, please," she begs. My hand works the toy with hers. The other is on my cock, and when Leigh's hand wraps around mine, both of use working together to find our mutual pleasure, I know my cum is going to be ripped out of my body if she doesn't get there soon.

"Get there, sweetheart. I'm going to paint your body with my cum, claim you in a way that will be permanently ingrained in your memory," I groan, watching as her body tightens, knowing she's coming on a toy, and if I weren't so fucking stubborn, it could be my cock she was choking instead.

"Phoenix." It's low and throaty, a rasp even. Her head is tipped back, eyes fluttering closed, hands tightening around my own as she finds her release. I hold back until she comes back to life, wanting her to watch as I do exactly what I said I would.

"You ready for me, Leigh, ready to watch as you push me over the edge?" I ask, keeping the toy inside her body, seeing if I can push another orgasm out of her as I glide my palm up and down, twisting along the way, gripping it tighter. Leigh's hands stay where they are, as if she's scared that this will all disappear once it's over.

"Come for me, Nix, come on me. I want to see you let go." Her eyes open, green with hazel-brown flecks floating around; they go back and forth in color. My balls are heavy, body ready to release its load. I watch as the first spurt of cum hits her smooth creamy skin, the hot fluid to her cooling skin that's dripping with perspiration.

"Leigh," I groan, taking my hand off my dick, letting my body finish what we started. I don't stop until her chest, stomach, and cunt are dripping with my cum.

"Jesus, that was so hot. If this is your idea of not having

foreplay, I vote we do it again as soon as possible." I sit back on my haunches after getting on my knees to come all over her body. "Or maybe we do that now. You're still hard. How is that even possible?"

I laugh. She has no ungodly idea what she's capable of, how she's looking at me like I'm her savior, naked before me. Nothing fucking compares. Nothing. "Oh, it's possible. Now, how about you go hop in the shower. I'll head to my place and do the same. Then we'll go make our rounds to get the girls, head to my folks' place, and later today, that talk we need to have will happen."

"Or you could shower here," she states. I slowly withdraw the toy from her body, watching as she clenches down on it, not ready to be done. That makes two of us, judging by the way my cock is refusing to deflate.

"Sweetheart, as much as I want that, I won't tempt myself. You naked is hard already. You naked and wet, I'd be completely fucked." I slide off the bed, unable to button my pants because my cock is still hard. My hand goes to hers once I'm standing. I notice she isn't grabbing for the first available item to rub my cum off her body.

"You can't blame a girl for trying." One of her hands is in mine, the other on my abdomen, making it hard to leave her. "Are you coming back over after you're ready, or am I coming to you?" It's on the top of my tongue to say, 'You're coming again.' Since I'm the one putting a stop to this when she's more than willing, I bite my tongue.

"I'll come to you." My hand covers hers on my stomach. I want another taste of her lips to hold me over until I'm back. Rosaleigh gives me what I'm after, lifting to the tips of her toes, mouth meeting mine, tongue seeking mine, and when I allow her to gain entrance, I take over, hand going to the back of her head, holding her where I want her as I twine my tongue with hers, not ending our kiss until both of us are breathless.

"Are you sure I can't convince you to stay?"

"Soon. Soon, you won't be able to get me to leave, even when you're sick of me." I press a kiss on her lips one last time, then step back and button up my jeans, leaving the last one undone to give my cock some breathing room, knowing I'll be putting my shirt on before I walk out of her house. I don't mind giving the neighbors something to talk about in the way of me leaving Rosaleigh's house in the morning. My hard cock, on the other hand, is entirely different.

"I'm not sure that will ever happen, but I'll see you in an hour." My cum is drying on her body, making me want to beat my own chest with the knowledge that Leigh doesn't mind it at all.

"Later, sweetheart." I reluctantly back out of her bedroom, doing so backwards so she's aware that this is not me walking away; it's me staying, no matter what happens.

14

ROSALEIGH

I'm never going to recover. My legs are still weak. If it weren't for wanting to prove to Nix that he could have more of me than he already had, I'd probably have begged him to carry me to the shower. And that was only with my favorite vibrator, the one that has dual motions on the shaft and the rabbit-like ears to work my clit. I can't even imagine what it would be like if Phoenix gave in and used his cock. One that I got a thorough look at—thick and long, the head bigger than Nix's length. It's the type you read about or watch porn to see, one you don't want anywhere near that one forbidden hole because you know it'll literally rip your ass apart.

I turn the water to piping hot, still walking around my bedroom and bathroom naked, a small phenomenon that never occurs when the house is full of all of us. Sadly, those days when they were little, didn't have a care in the world, are long gone. So, what do I do? I luxuriate in the fact that my legs, breasts, lips, and center are deliciously sore as I go out to the kitchen to make a hot cup of coffee to enjoy in the shower while the water finally heats up. Another task to take care of—the hot water heater is on its last leg. One of these days, it'll finally quit producing the liquid inferno that we James girls love so much, and that will be a day we literally freeze to death while we argue who broke it. True to Nix's word, Rory texted me last night that she was going to sleep and said she loved me. My night owl Emmy texted me back around one o'clock this morning, judging by the unread text that's appearing on my lock screen. I make a cup of coffee, convincing myself not to pick up the phone and call Ophelia. "Don't do it. She's three hours behind you, probably conked out asleep. And it's not like you can tell her about the orgasms her own brother gave you," I tell the coffee pot, tapping my fingers while it gets the water hot, too. Everything and anything are going to take its sweet time when it comes to making my beverage and shower hot. Finally, the dark chocolate caffeine goodness percolates, dripping into my cup. I grab my favorite creamer out of the fridge. Yes, cold creamer in my scalding-hot coffee is my jam. Sue me. I'm sure I'll be reheating my cup in the microwave at least twice, too. I doctor my coffee up, sugar-free creamer that Rory has told me is horrible for my body, and I'd be better off putting two teaspoons of sugar in me instead. That's for another day, another time, when I'm not running on fumes. I cut back on my wine. Isn't that enough for now?

I take my first sip as I walk back through the kitchen and hallway. The slight pull of Phoenix's cum drying on my body with every movement is a reminder of how he had no problem shooting his load all over me. Nix said it was a way to claim me. Little does he know I want to be claimed, well, once we get a few things out of the way. Having a child with him is one of them. While it made my heart melt, my ovaries tingle, and bring up the thought of maybe having a boy this time around, it also means starting over. I'm still young. My girls are older, though, and that's a lot. How would the logistics work? Would we rip the girls out of the only home they've ever known besides Ya-Ya's and Papou's house? There's so much to think about, but I won't deny him that option if it's something we can both agree on.

The shower water still isn't hot when I walk back into my bathroom, no steam is billowing from the stall, and there is no way in hell I'd stick my foot, let alone my body, in the cold, frigid water. Here I stand, still coming down from a Phoenix high, wishing he had stayed. I would have promised to keep my hands to myself with my fingers crossed behind my back because there's no way I actually would have succeeded. His body is too delicious to not touch, lick, or taste. And that small taste, not even from the source but mixed with my skin, it was a tease, and I'm going to do everything in my power to make Nix lose control.

"Finally." I can feel the room getting hotter, so I move the shower curtain to the side, cup of coffee in my hand, placing it on the built-in shelf, once again not letting it go to waste. I grab the clip, shocked that it's actually where I left it because I'm known for leaving them all around the house. Rory rarely uses them, preferring to use hair ties, keeping it around her wrist constantly. Emmy is into big silk-like scrunchies that she loses constantly. The hot water beats on my back. I'm unable to turn into the water, unwilling to lose what I have left of Nix just yet. Call me crazy, but I'm not ready. Instead, I close my eyes and reach for my cup of coffee without opening them. The same routine for years now when I have the time. I smile at how I've gone through a shit ton of turmoil through the years. A home life that wasn't the most ideal, then starting a family entirely too young. Totally worth it, though. Marrying the man I thought was going to be my forever, him walking out like we were disposable, and then I had my name tarnished. I didn't let it keep me down. There was no way I could fall into a pit of despair. As much as I would have loved to drop to my bed, bury myself under the covers, and sleep the pain away, I had two girls who needed their mother. Coming back swinging was my only option.

"Leigh, how are you still in the shower, woman?" I'm knocked out of my moment and jump backwards, coffee hitting my chest since I picked up the cup to have another sip, and under the water I go.

"Phoenix Drakos, I'm going to take your code to my damn house away. I literally just got in here, and now my coffee is ruined, my hair is wet, and so am I!" I exclaim, annoyed that now his cum that was dried on my body is being washed away. A few more minutes, that's all I was hoping for.

"Fuck yeah, you are. What have you been doing the last thirty minutes?" He keeps the shower curtain open and leans against the wall, hair wet, freshly shaven in the areas he's not growing a beard, wearing a fresh shirt and pair of jeans. Nix, with his piercing blue eyes, looks utterly unashamed as he licks his lower lip, watching as the water cascades down my body.

"Waiting for the water to get hot since no one's used it since sometime yesterday, made my now ruined cup of coffee, and then I was enjoying my time without two girls barging in. It looks like I got a better surprise. Care to drop the clothes and join me?" I grab the soap, ready to hand it to him.

"I'll make you another cup, and I'm not joining you. Yet. Think you can be ready in twenty minutes? Emmy texted me when she couldn't get ahold of you. She's done hanging out with her friend and is ready to go see Ya-Ya, her words verbatim," Nix tells me, completely sounding like my youngest child. She's a social butterfly for all of maybe twenty-four hours if you're lucky, then she's ready to be with her family.

"Fine, I'll hurry up. I swear the one day I get to take a shower in peace will be the day." I thrust my cup of coffee at him, letting him know it's a necessity if he wants me to move my ass.

"Ma'am, yes ma'am." He takes the cup, but not without looking me up and down. A groan works its way up his throat, and when I think he's going to give in to what I so clearly am willing to give him, he turns on his heel and walks out.

15

NIX

"Mammy llama, looking good there, lady fox," Emmy greets Rosaleigh once my truck is in park at her friend's house. Next up is Rory. She was slower to respond, enjoying her time, going with the flow.

"Dear God, Emmy Lou, it's like you haven't seen me out of my work or house clothes before. Did you have a good time, peanut butter?" You'd almost feel like a third wheel if you weren't used to the James girls having their own conversations. I've been around enough years to know it's how they interact.

"It was fun. We watched scary movies and ate our weight in pizza. You would be surprised, I laid off the ice cream! You think Ya-Ya and Papou will have dessert today?" Emmy may sometimes act older than her ten years around the sun, but give the girl an ounce of sugar, and she'll ask for a cup.

"It's your funeral if you ask her," I interject.

"Hey, Nix, and no thanks. That's why I'm asking you two. I'm not ready for her to chase me out of the kitchen with whatever she can find to pretend to use as a weapon."

"Hiya, girlie. If Ya-Ya doesn't have dessert, I'm pretty sure we can convince your mom to stop for some ice cream. You buckled?" I ask, putting the truck in reverse and heading to our next destination before heading to my folks' house.

"I am now." She kisses her mom's cheek, then mine, plopping down in the middle of the backseat since Rory isn't in the truck to complain that Emmy is crowding her space. That's why she's taking advantage of the situation to be able to sit in her favorite spot if she's not riding shot gun.

"And how many times have you taken the girls for coffee, donuts, ice cream, and who knows what this week?" I'm not touching that subject. Rosaleigh would not like the answer, and after hearing the reason why she's been cutting back, well, I'd do a shit ton more if it meant she's no longer attached to Douchebag David.

"I plead the fifth," I reply under my breath. Leigh huffs out a laugh, dropping the subject. That doesn't mean Emmy stops talking for the next five minutes about what movies they watched, how one of the horror films looked fake, the second one was better, and then how they watched a Disney princess movie to fall asleep to.

"What did you two get up to last night?" I'm at the curb of where Rory spent the night, both girls preferring to hang with their friend they've known since kindergarten. Small town life; you gotta love it. That's not was has me and Leigh looking at one another, wondering how the hell Emmy could figure anything out. "Obliviously, Mom stayed home last night. Lame, dude, lame." I turn in my seat to get a look at her. Keeping a straight face is damn near impossible. "Tracked you, Momsies. Nix, we need to get you on our circle. Then we'll all know where everyone is at any given time."

"You and your sister track me entirely too much. Sometimes I wonder who's the mom and who's the child when it comes to that app." Rosaleigh has a look of relief on her face, probably having the same worry I did. If someone told the girls we spent the night together before we had a chance to sit down, figure out how we were going to make this work, I'd have been pissed as fuck and someone would have felt my wrath.

"Hey, hey, hey. Thanks for picking Emmy up first. We were still being couch potatoes. What did I miss?" Rory hops into the truck, looking at all three of us, then telling Emmy, "Move over, sister. I love you, but not enough for you to sit on top of me on a car ride."

"The sass level is at a hundred today. Get it out now and don't annoy Nix too much before we arrive at Ya-Ya's and Papou's. Emmy, leave the poor man alone. I'm sure the last thing he needs is you two stalking his location," Leigh replies, picking up her travel mug filled with coffee that I made for her after ruining her first cup.

"Oh, I love that idea. Honestly, it would help in times when Mom has to stay at work late and we don't know if you're at the shop or at home." I hear the distinct click of Rory's seatbelt, allowing me to get this show on the road. By the time we finally make it to my parents' house, Leigh is going to be hopped up on caffeine without food and the girls are going to be ready for their second if not third meal of the day.

"You two, let the man have a moment without you harassing him, okay?" My eyes are on the road, a smirk on my face, enjoying the way the James women have no problem talking every situation out.

"Add me to the circle, Em." I grab my phone out of the cup holder and hand it to her. She knows the code, and I've got nothing to hide. The girls might not clue in yet, but they're doing me a favor more than they know. It won't be long until Rory is out with a group of friends, going to movies, and more boys are sniffing around as it is. Next up, it'll be Emmy, and fuck if that doesn't do something inside my chest. I'm not prepared to watch my girls grow up to be young women, that's for damn sure.

"Right on! Nix is the best!" The rearview mirror shows Em raising her hand above her head as she does a fist bump. I shake my head at her theatrics, then look briefly at Leigh. She mouths, *I'm sorry.* There's absolutely nothing to be sorry about, and if we had the chance this morning to talk to the girls, I know exactly where my hand would be, reassuring her that I'll take all three of their brand of crazy, anytime, anywhere.

16

NIX

"My babies!" That's how mom greets us when we walk into their house, a small two-bedroom home in a retirement community for fifty-five plus. They decided to downsize once I bought the shop, wanting more activities with other people their age. The one drawback is they aren't as close to Rosaleigh and me anymore. Our town of Abalee in Georgia didn't have anything like what they were looking for, which took them to the next town over, making it a twenty-minute drive instead of them being across the street for the girls. "I haven't seen you in so long. Let me look at you, Rory, so tall now. And Emmy, my goodness, look at all that hair. You know, you're the spitting image of your momma. It's like looking at her clones. Wouldn't you agree, Phoenix?" Leigh and I don't get a hug or a kiss, not even a hello. My mother is in full-blown Ya-Ya mode. No one and nothing is going to stand in her way.

"They are. Sometimes, one of them will say something, and I'm not sure if it's Leigh I'm talking to or one of the girls." Rosaleigh didn't come into our lives until she was almost fifteen. That doesn't mean the girls aren't following right in her footsteps in the beauty department.

"Come here, Leigh-Leigh." My dad isn't getting the time he wants with Rory or Emmy anytime soon, so he may as well give Rosaleigh his attention. As for me, I may as well be chopped liver. That's okay, though. Seeing them with my family is all I could ever want. I lean against the wall, watching and waiting, biding my time. It's been a while since Mom and Dad saw the girls because of Leigh's work schedule. As for me, I was here the other day. I also call my father anytime there's a new car that makes its way into the shop that I know he'd appreciate.

It's then that I see my dad is looking at me over Rosaleigh's head. I got my height from him, definitely not my mom with her small frame. He may be hitting his late fifties, but that's not slowing him down any, and judging by the look my father's giving me, he knows I've finally made my move when it comes to making Leigh mine. I nod, giving him that reassurance. His head does the same, the gray coming in more and more as every year passes.

"We missed you, Ya-Ya. Madre, quit hogging Papou." Emmy moves out of my mom's arms, ready to share the love. Rory does the same, but instead of going where Emmy is, she stands next to me, head resting on my shoulder. My arm wraps around her. I'm tempted to ask if something is wrong, but I remember Ophelia at this age. Talking was out of the question most of the time, unless I bribed her with ice cream. I'm sure there will be time this week for us to have a spare moment together.

"Well, you were hogging Ya-Ya, so hush, child," Rosaleigh jokes back with Emmy. The two swap out girls, while Rory still sticks by my side, and that boy drama her sister spoke about the other day is making me think that this is bigger than even Leigh knows about.

"You guys hungry? Of course, you're hungry. You don't come over not to eat. Papou and I made your favorites." That gets Rory's attention.

"Greek salad with extra olives and feta?" That comes from Emmy. The girl has a weird obsession with vegetables and cheese of any kind.

"I'm hoping for Pastitsio," Rory whispers to me, talking about the Greek lasagna dish. Truth be told, I could go for about anything. The coffee and protein bar I had at my house are definitely wearing off.

"Is that your favorite?" The others are moving into the living room, dispersing. Leigh and Mom into the kitchen. Emmy and my dad in the living room, probably to show her the latest car magazine he picked up.

"It is, well, besides souvlaki. Those two meals are amazing. Don't tell Mom, though. She tries, but cooking is not her forte. She can make an awesome sandwich that is out of this world amazing, but a real meal? It's burnt nine times out of ten." Rosaleigh's attention span in the kitchen is that of a gnat unless it's easy type of meals, coffee, and of the beverage variety.

"Your secret is safe with me. You good, sweetheart?" I

can't help it; something pulls at me to at least ask her in case
it's worse than she's letting on.

"I'm okay. Mom deserves a man like you, Nix. She does
everything, never complains. I see how tired she is, and boys,
well, boys are stupid, except you. You're the best there is." I
press a kiss to the side of her head.

"Boys are most assuredly stupid. We'll get back to that
when you need an ear to listen. Your mom deserves it all,
and she'll get it. Now, let's go see what we can get our hands
on. I'm starving. Your mom is living on caffeine, so you know
she's devouring everything in sight, and if we want any food,
we better get our asses moving." I walk her toward the
kitchen.

"Phoenix Stephen Drakos, did you just say a word that
shouldn't be said around a young lady? I'm going to put soap
in your mouth." Mom's got ears like a hawk.

"Uh-oh, you're in trouble now, Nix. You got full-named.
That spells trouble, so you're on your own." Rory leaves my
side, moving to where her mom is standing at the counter,
stuffing food in her mouth as fast as she can. I should have
made Leigh some breakfast while she was showering. Next
time, I'll be sure to do that.

"Traitor," I tease Rory, then walk to my mother to say
hello.

"Hey, Mom." I bend down to kiss her cheek as we hug.
She's got her lips next to my ear, whispering to me low so
only the two of us can hear, and I know that's the case. Leigh,
and Rory, along with Emmy, are basically deaf compared to
Mom and me.

"My boy, you've got a great treasure in front of you. Make

this official. I want my girls to have the love of a real man. I admired what you did years ago. Now is the time. They're the happiest they've ever been, and I know it has everything to do with you." I close my eyes. She's right. Of course, she is. There's no denying it.

"Not messing around, not ever again." It's not the time to go more in depth, not with everyone milling around. Anyone could sneak up on our conversation.

"Good. You cuss in front of my granddaughters again, I'm going to smack you." Mom pats my cheek, winking as she does.

"I thought you were going to put soap in my mouth?" I tease her as I pull away, heading to where the girls are currently scarfing down cheese, olives, meats, and whatever they can before Emmy and my dad walk in.

"You going to save any for me, or is this a free for all?" Leigh doesn't respond, too busy chewing her food.

"Nix, we're women. Food is life. And you never mess with a woman when she's eating." I go to grab an olive. Rory does a fake growl, Leigh snorts, and I chuckle.

"Dinner's ready. The three of you get out of the appetizer, or you'll ruin my meal. Rory requested dinner last time she was here, so it's her turn. Nix, get the casserole out of the oven. Adonis, help the girls set the table." Mom claps her hands together, and we do her bidding, all of us prepared to do anything when it comes to one of her delicious dinners, even if we're being prodded like cattle to do what she says.

17

ROSALEIGH

"Pick up, please pick up." I'm calling my best friend, my sister in a way that is thicker than blood. The phone keeps ringing, once, twice, three times, then another. I'm worried she's working on a Sunday night. Ophelia calls me a workaholic. Hello, pot, meet kettle. It rings yet another time. One more ring, and it'll go to voicemail. I'm unsure of who I'll talk to if she doesn't answer, more than likely myself. We reverted to our usual Nix and Leigh selves once the girls were in the truck, meaning no hand holding, the palm of his hand was no longer holding the inside of my thigh, and talking freely was out of the question, too, not that it lasted long. A quick five-minute trip to get Emmy made it impossible to talk to him about how to navigate this relationship we agreed on. Alright, he claimed me. It was the claiming of a man you'd read about in one of the novels who has a long-haired hero, shirtless, overly muscled on its cover, holding a woman tightly to his body.

"Ophelia Drakos, it's about damn time you answered. I'm having an emergency over here. What were you doing, woman?" I demand once she picks up the phone, not giving her a chance to say hello.

"Give a woman a break, will you? I was unlocking the door, trying to get inside the freaking house." She blows out a puff of air into the phone. I laugh, envisioning Fif with her oversized bag, phone buried at the bottom, keys probably in a spot she didn't remember putting it, cussing in every imaginable language she can.

"It's ten o'clock here. Are you telling me you're just now getting home from work at seven on a Sunday?" I ask, trying to question her without coming out and asking it blatantly.

"Work dinner. May as well have been on a job. It sucked so bad, the food was horrible and miniscule. You should see how these Hollywood celebrities and billionaires eat. It's one asparagus, a piece of meat the size of your thumb, and a dallop of potatoes." I could never imagine the lifestyle she lives. Don't get me wrong, she rocks it, but dealing with the snotty people Ophelia does, it's a no for me.

"So, I guess telling you we had dinner with your parents would be torture?" I'm sitting in my bedroom, unable to go out on the back porch without being too loud with the girls' rooms in the back of the house. Our house is a true split floor plan, allowing me to be obnoxious on the phone with Fif, which happens anytime we're on the phone late at night.

"You're a bitch. Please tell me you ate enough for two, like you did when you were pregnant with my goddaughters." Ophelia's the girls' aunt and godmother all in one, the best of both worlds. Always there for them no matter the time or day, even if she's on set making sure whatever celebrity she's working with is dressed to the nines.

"I ate like I was pregnant with Emmy. Nix helped as well, and you know he can put down some food. Which, by the way, we need to talk about the Nix and Rosaleigh situation." I should have brought a glass of wine; maybe it would calm the nerves currently swirling in my lower abdomen. I'm not even sure why I have them. Before I met David, Ophelia and I would lie on our backs, the carpet cushioning us, legs swinging up in the air, hoping that one day, we would be related. And while yes, I had a secret crush on her brother for a time, I knew there was no going there. Nix always kept me at a distance. When I met his best friend, the David thing developed from there. Now David is gone, and Nix, who has really stepped up even more than he was before, is here, clearly to stay, too.

"Girlfriend, you are the only one who didn't see Nix has had hearts in his eyes when it came to you for, well, ever." I pull my knees up to my chest and rest my chin on top of it, inhaling a deep breath of air, holding it in before slowly releasing it.

"Yeah, I really kept my blinders on a little too long, didn't I," I state even if it does seem like a question, one I know Fif won't answer. I think back to earlier today when Nix had no problem draping his hand over my lap beneath the dinner table, the tablecloth hiding how he would rub my thigh every now and then. How Rory went right to him, and I watched them have a conversation like they've done all her life. David never did that, never spent time in the garage working on a car only to have his girls around. My girls had a father who wasn't a father. When it all came down to it, Phoenix was there, to help me teach them how to ride bikes, at every school performance because David was working. It's always been Phoenix. Always.

"Okay, now that those are off, finally, don't think I'm not dying to tell you I told you so." A snort leaves me, clearing the heaviness. Ophelia has stated that a multitude of times and every chance she could get.

"How humble of you. The problem is that I'm full of what-ifs. What if he wants a child, but I don't? What if he wants marriage? Which, by the way, I'm still technically married, and this isn't that sister-wife show. Then there's the house. Would we live across the street from one another? There are so many what-ifs, and while last night with your brother was amazing,"—she makes the gagging noise, one where you know she's mimicking the finger down the throat, little shit—"I'm not saying what happened. I love you; I'd never subject you to it, promise. There's just so much that's been left unsaid."

Ophelia is quiet on the other end of the line; so am I, for that matter. I can see myself with Nix, no doubt about it. Even if it's been less than a year since David rocked me to my core, the truth of the matter is our marriage fell apart long before that. The lack of intimacy, us coming and going at opposite times of days, obviously David was working elsewhere besides the sheriff's department, a single mom yet married, make it make sense.

"Calm your tits, first and foremost. Pour yourself a glass of wine or give yourself an orgasm, stat. The last thing anyone needs is for you to have a coronary. Then, after you do a deep breathing session with your toy or guzzle the wine I know my brother stocked you up on, go to him. The only person who can answer your questions is across the street."

"Why are you always right? An orgasm isn't necessary, by the way." Laughter bubbles out of me, trying to get a rise out of Ophelia.

"Ugh, you're so gross. I do not want details, Rosaleigh!"

"Fine, I won't. Do you want to tell me why you're miserable out in California yet aren't willing to come home?" I can hear the weariness in her voice. This isn't the first time we've spoken this week. Earlier, it was me staying up till one o'clock in the morning to answer her call. Fif was spitting mad, cussing her boss up a storm while I listened, having no idea what happened, only that he was a conniving asshole who thinks he farts unicorns.

"The money. If it weren't for the money, I'd be home in Abalee. Two more years, max. If not, I'll call it quits and beg for help. I was so stupid, following a boy out here, getting into debt by transferring from one school to the next. I love what I do; I do not love the hefty student loan debt or the ridiculous amount of rent I'm paying." She stayed home until Emmy was born, then it was time for my best friend to spread her wings, though California wasn't where I thought she'd land.

"I know the money isn't as good back here. The option is always open for you to move in with me. Rent would be cheap, and you could probably be out of debt sooner." I'd offer her some of the cash I put away for the probability of a divorce attorney, but I know she wouldn't take it, and the need to disassociate from David is real.

"It's dumb, I know. Also, speaking of, Rory called. I'm not sure if she's told you, but that stupid boy Tyler—obviously, don't tell her I told you this—anyways, they were in that proverbial talking stage teenage kids think is so fun these days. He asked her to send a nude. Our girl is obviously too smart for that, so she blocked him on everything—social media, texts, and calls. It still fucked with her head. Nix doesn't know, and I'd suggest not telling him, or you might need bail money."

"Nix won't need bail money. I will. That little cocksucker. Jesus, Fif, she didn't even talk to me about this. I mean, I'm glad she talked to you, but damn if that doesn't make me worry that she's not talking about other things, keeping more and more in." I hit my forehead on my knees, upset with myself, pissed at that fuckwad of a kid. Mostly, I'm upset with myself, though.

"Eh, it takes a village. Rory's got a good head on her shoulders. Maybe hang with her for a bit tomorrow. Guaranteed she'll open up, even if it's while you attempt to cook some sort of unburnt dinner." She's not wrong. Usually, we'd have the weekend to hang out. Rory going to a friend's house last night made things a bit difficult. I'll be home all day tomorrow. That means the girls will get a ride to school, I'll pick them up after, and do the same routine for sports. A lot of opportunities to have some girl time while we wait for Emmy to get out of school.

"You're right, on everything, like usual. Have I mentioned nobody likes a know-it-all?"

"Maybe once or twice. Now, go get your man before it gets too late. Also, I'm going to make the biggest bowl of cereal, shower, then conk out." Ophelia yawns. Whenever you think you have it rough, someone else has it worse. At least here in Abalee, I'm surrounding by people who love me and the girls. She's in California by herself without her family.

"Fruit Loops, I hope. I love you. Thank you for listening to me ramble," I tell her while trying to come up with a game plan if the divorce attorney doesn't take me for a ride.

"Always and forever. I love you, and I'm always here." We hang up. I head to my closet, already in my short and tank pajama set, this one not as old and threadbare as last night's version, grab my robe that's bright and cheerful, and do what my best friend suggests. It's now Operation Talk to Nix.

18

ROSALEIGH

I f Ophelia could see me now, she probably would have told me to at least make myself more presentable. My once messy bun that was on top of my head is falling out, lopsided, I'm sure. The robe I grabbed is a few years old, practically threadbare for how much I use it, since it's well-loved, well-used, and a splurge that I know Rory and Emmy saved up to have Fif give me for my birthday one year. The flowers are vibrant, the material is luxurious, and even when it becomes holey, I still won't give it up. It's the shoes that are currently on my feet that have me questioning what the hell I'm doing over here without looking in a mirror. I mean, the outfit is what it is, but the rainbow-colored rubber shoes that have all kinds of charm, like things pressed into the top of the holes. Why Rory and Emmy insist on these ugly, colossal clog-like shoes, I'll never know.

I attempt to tame what I'm sure is my wild hair and straighten my robe after walking across the street and going up the few steps Nix has. My front porch has pots full of flowers, two small chairs, and a table, and my flowerbeds are lush and mature, the grass is green and well maintained because I refuse to let it go. Plus, working outside in my yard is an escape from reality—my mind turns off, there's nothing except me, the lawn equipment, the sun beating down on my body, and my headphones. Phoenix's yard is not that—cut grass, zero plants, a chair that has seen better days, and that's it.

"Here goes nothing." Nix has a doorbell I could and should use, but I don't bother pressing the button, unless in the rare occurrence he's asleep, unlike the person standing on the other side of his wood door, knocking. Another thought goes through my mind, like *Oh, I don't know. Maybe I should have called or texted him instead of just showing up unannounced.* Plus, it's not like I'm making a lot of noise as it is. I knock one more time, a little harder this go-around. If he doesn't answer the door, well, I'll head back to my house, wait until tomorrow. Since I have the day off, I can always get ahold of him, maybe bring him a sandwich and have lunch with him at the shop.

"Leigh. Jesus, sweetheart, you scared the shit out of me. I thought it was one of the girls knocking on the door because something was wrong," Nix answers the door His hair looks like he's run his fingers through it countless times, and he's shirtless, wearing only a pair of flannel pajama pants. My gaze is taking the entirety of him in. It never gets old, not when I was a teenager who barely knew what a man like him was capable of, and definitely not now that I know given the opportunity Nix will be mine if I say the words.

"Um, yeah. This wasn't the best planning on my part. Would it help matters any if I said this was partly Ophelia's plan?" I shrug my shoulders. The belt around my waist loosens. A bad habit of mine is just loping it over the ends, pulling it tight; obviously, it tends to unravel when you do that. Nix must take notice. One moment I'm on his doorstep, the next his arm is wrapped around my waist beneath my now open robe, skin to skin, a heated touch, my fingers pressing firmly to him as he picks me up. The door is slammed shut, my back is pressed against it, and the only thing I can hear is our combined breathing along with my heart beating through my veins.

"Remind me to send her flowers." He doesn't mess around. The hand that closed the door holds the back of my head as his lips and tongue take mine, the fresh mint taste with the undertone that's so uniquely Nix consuming me; there's no other word for it. My hands are at his lower abdomen, trailing upwards until I'm pressing on his pecs, nails digging in. The questioning that was going through my brain earlier, all the what-ifs, should we, could we, do we, they all evaporate. Will the navigation of a new relationship be hard? I'm sure it'll be ten times harder than anything I did with David. Where I was young and basically followed his lead, it's different with Nix. He consumes every depth of my being.

"Phoenix." He lifts away from my lips, moving until his lips are a whisper away from my ear. I so badly want to lift my leg over his hip, spreading myself open for him, to feel him against me even if it's only for a moment.

"Love you in my house. Dreamed of the day you'd come

to me. And the way you look right now, it's a dream come to life." He bends at the knees, his front completely against mine, and I kind of hate myself for having my hands on his chest when I know that I could have our bodies fused to each other.

"God, yes, more." His hand that was on my lower back slides inside my shorts, grasping the cheek of my ass, lifting me in his arms. My legs automatically wrap around him, and this time, I slide my hands up until they're on his shoulders. Nix's legs spread my thighs. The length of him is hard, thick, and heavy. My mind is only focused on the sensations he's pulling from my body.

"Fuck, sweetheart. I can feel you. It's all for me. Fuck yeah, it's all for me." He swivels his hips, the head of his cock lays claim to my slit, and my head tips back. "Are you ready to make this official?" Phoenix asks while playing my body like a violin. Every touch, every groan, every whisper plays together. I'm strung so tight that one more flex of his hips, nip of his teeth near my ear, and I know my body will sing.

"Yes, we still have to talk, but I'm all in, Nix. All freaking in." The fingers that were gripping my ass move until two of his digits are at my entrance, so close yet so far away.

"And we'll have that talk after you come for me." He thrusts his fingers deep inside me. How that's possible, I have no idea. Maybe he's double jointed or flexible? It doesn't really matter. All that does matter is the way he's grinding his length along the seam of my pussy, his head hitting my clit with every movement, along with his fingers. I'm already on the cusp of my orgasm. I bite my lower lip to drown out the noise, so used to having to be quiet in my bed that I don't even realize I'm doing it until Phoenix is sucking at my lip, pulling it out of the way, soothing the indentations from my teeth with his tongue. "One day soon, I'm going to hear you scream my name, Leigh." He swallows my moan with his mouth as I come apart, only for him to pick up the pieces, like he's always done.

"Every time we're together, I think it's the best I've ever had, then you one-up the experience, and I can't tell which way is up and which way is down," I admit, eyes opening slowly. Phoenix pulls his fingers out of my center, holding me up with his firm thighs.

"Greatest gift you've ever given me, sweetheart. Those words, you coming for me, making me break my rules." I watch as he does something I least expect. His fingers that were inside me are slick with wetness, and I watch as he sucks them into his mouth, a growl rumbling in his chest. My core clenches. I just came, yet watching how he reacts to my taste, it makes me greedy for more.

"Shit, Leigh, soon. It's going to be my head buried between your thighs, tasting you right from the source. That can't happen right now. Let me get some clothes on. I'll walk you back home, and we'll talk on your porch in case the girls wake up." I lower my legs as Nix steps back, hands on my hips to hold me steady. I swear I'm going to have to start doing some kind of leg and hip exercises to get used to the way he has me stretched out in various positions. It's going to be necessary.

"I'd like that, a lot," I tell him, noticing the outline of his is cock is on display through his pajama pants.

"Cute shoes," he teases. It's then that I notice I'm no

longer wearing the clogs. They're haphazardly on the floor from being kicked off my feet.

"They're hideous. I wasn't going to ruin my slippers in the street." Which is part of the truth; the other is that I was in such a rush to get to him, I wasn't thinking about looks.

"I'll be right back. Don't go anywhere." I roll my eyes at his command. It's like he's forgotten I'm the one who came to him. I'm not ready to leave without him any time soon.

19

NIX

True to my word, it only takes a me a few minutes to change out of my pajama pants; not that I wear them to bed, a preference that I'm sure will be changing once Rosaleigh and I have our talk. I'll be around the girls more, and I don't want them to see certain things. Fuck, that'd be hard to even begin to explain. I grab a pair of sweats out of my drawer, strip out of the pants, not at all annoyed that the reason I'm changing them is because Leigh got herself off on my cloth-covered cock, leaving her wetness in her wake. Once those are on, I grab a cotton shirt with the name of the shop emblazoned on the front. It's faded from years of wear while at work and home. I'm walking back into the living room in under two minutes. If I had more time, I probably would have taken care of my aching cock. That will have to wait because we've been away from Rosaleigh's house long enough. I grab my phone, pocket it, and sweep the area for the woman who's been mine since the moment I met her. Even if she didn't know it at the time or through the years, too many years to count but worth it in the end; I'd have waited longer to have Rosaleigh wake up in my arms.

"You ready?" I ask as I walk up behind her where she's staring at the frames that are lining the sofa table. There are a few of the girls growing up through the years, another with the whole family, the James' included, minus Douchebag David. The one she's got her eyes locked on, not saying a word, is the most recent of the four of us taken last month. It was a rare Sunday off for Leigh. The girls asked if we could go to a concert that was being held in the park. Emmy was trying to take a selfie with all of us, struggling because her arm wasn't long enough, then asked a passerby if they'd snap a picture. It's probably my favorite one of the bunch. Rosaleigh didn't have dark circles under her eyes; she was the young and carefree woman while being a mom at the same time. My mom being that mom saw the picture, had it printed and framed for me to add to the collection.

"I am. All these years, and the man who I was meant to be with is the one who has always had my back." My hands are on her shoulders, body locking tight when her words sink in. If there were ever any doubt in my mind that she still had any kind of feelings for Douchebag David, they'd be gone. Leigh saying that only solidifies it further, on top of the little tidbits of information she's been dolling out, like not having sex for well over a year, what she said right now, and that one time she spoke under her breath about being married to the wrong man.

"Always, Rosaleigh, fucking always." I kiss the top of her head and pull her way from the pictures, our fingers threaded through each other's. I'm ready to have this conversation, to not have anything stand in our way, which is why I'm practically dragging her through the door. I could have slowed down, and when she took two steps for my one, I was tempted to pick her up to get her there faster. I barely fucking refrained. And when we make it across the street, I breathe a sigh of relief. There's something to be said when a man of the law is crookeder than a dog's dick and runs like the coward he is, and still is. It makes you worry night and day not about if but when he comes back, because if there's one thing I know about my douchebag ex-best friend, it's that he'll make an appearance when we least expect it.

"Go check on the girls, sweetheart. I'm going to grab us a couple of bottles of waters and meet you back here on the front porch," I tell Rosaleigh once I've inputted the code to her door, letting my hand go slack in hers, noticing she squeezes mine once before doing the same.

"I'll be right back." I close the door, expecting her to head in the direction of the bedrooms. That's not Rosaleigh, though. Her cool hands touch my cheeks, cupping them, and I dip down when she starts to stand on the tips of her toes.

"You're the best man there ever could be, Phoenix Drakos, and I'm never going to let you go." My eyes close, and I breathe in her scent, soaking in the words. My chest expands with male pride. When I open them, I press my lips to hers, keeping it short so she can make sure all is right in the bedrooms down the hall.

"Right back at you, sweetheart." We pull away from one another. The moment she turns around, her going one way while I'm going to be veering off the other, my hand slaps her ass lightly. The saucy grin she tosses over her shoulder only bolsters what I feel for this woman. I head to the kitchen. Clearly, Rosaleigh was settled for the night and didn't bother turning on any extra lights on her way out the door. Judging by Rory's shoes Leigh had on her feet, she was going for something quick and easy. I notice the house is picked up along the way to the kitchen. Rosaleigh likes things put in their place at the end of every night, especially on a Sunday when she knows Mondays are always a pain in the ass. I open the fridge and see she's got the girls' lunches packed in brown paper sacks. Neither of them can be trusted with lunchboxes, haven't since their younger years. After they went through three a piece in one school year, she was over it. This way, all they have to do is throw away their trash. I smile. Rosaleigh has it going on—the girls, the house, the job, and now she'll have me.

"All is good with the girls. They haven't moved since I checked on them before I left to go to your house," Leigh says quietly as she comes back into the kitchen. I've got the bottles of water in my hand, a smile still plastered on my face.

"The girls always could sleep like the dead. It doesn't matter if a fire alarm were going off; they'd still be conked out. You wanna talk on the couch or on the front porch?" I ask, slowly walking toward her, drinks in hand. Leigh has lost the shoes, and on her feet now are slippers, the ones that have some kind of fluffy material, stylish and cute like the woman herself.

"Front porch, just in case. Plus, there are things a mother

does not want her kids to know about." My hand goes to her lower back as we walk back out the door we just came through. I watch as she slides the deadbolt out. That way, the door is cracked for not only us but the girls. The only bad part about this situation is that the furniture on the front porch isn't like the back patio or the comfort of a couch. We're in separate chairs, and a table is set between the two. That's why once Leigh is settled in her chair, I move mine closer, my ass to the seat, and I pull up her legs so they're on my thighs.

"Alright, I know you have some things you want to say, but before that happens, I'm going to make sure you're aware that nothing you tell me will deter me." I don't tack on how long I've been waiting on her or the way I know without a shadow of a doubt how Douchebag David swindled her into the kids and marriage aspect of her life.

"I'm seeing that," she says with a smile. I uncap the bottle of water for her, holding it out, then do the same for myself, giving Rosaleigh time to gather her thoughts. I watch as she takes a deep gulp of the water, throat working as she does. Visions of her on her knees, my cock in her mouth, assault me. It would be my cum she'd be swallowing instead of the water. Fuck, it's impossible to keep my cock from getting hard when I'm around her.

"Anyways, I guess I should tell you my worries first. Not that there are a lot, but it still needs to be said, like for instance children. Do you want them? I mean, besides my girls?" I can't tell if she's taking that off the table to potentially happen, or if she's asking because there's a piece of

Rosaleigh that wanted a houseful of kids when she was younger.

"Leigh, you gotta know your girls might not be my blood, but they're mine, just like you are. Do I like the thought of adding to our family? Fuck yes, especially the practicing part, but I'm good either way, sweetheart." Not a complete yes or no. Honestly, I'd love nothing more than for her to carry our child, to see her round and pregnant knowing it was me this time who made Leigh that way.

"Well, that's not very helpful. I never did get my tubes tied. Um, David did that, so I didn't see any reason." She makes the scissor cutting gesture with her two fingers. I guess that bag of dicks did one good deed.

"What else you got that we need to hash out?" My cock was settling down but rears its head, knowing that Leigh isn't shut down for good. Finding out if she's on anything to prevent a pregnancy is next on my agenda. I'll be doing a little snooping here and there.

"Well, we have the divorce stuff that needs to be handled. As soon as you talk to Eli, I'm going to get the ball rolling on that front. The need to be rid of David and his shit completely is a necessity. Plus, it feels weird to start something between the two of us without at least starting the process. Of course, it could take a long freaking time if he somehow protests it. That would require him coming back, and with every major agency looking for him, let's just say he was stupid as it is, but that would just be plain dumb." I take a sip of my water then set it down on the table before placing my hand back on her legs, needing to be touching her in some way.

"Seems like it's all ironed out. Nothing in this conversation so far is remotely bad, sweetheart. I will tell you this now, though. It'll be me taking you to the attorney's office. I'm not saying that I need to be in the office with you during the consult; I'll stay in the waiting room, but you're not alone in this, not now and not ever. Anything else?" Rosaleigh has questions; I've got the answers. She'll stew in this shit if she doesn't get it all out, not that she couldn't ask me anything at any given time. That's not her, though. Instead, she eternalizes it, so much like Rory in that aspect; it's when she finally lets it bubble over that you need to worry.

"I think that's it, though if we add to our family, we're going to need a bigger home. Oh, and there's that whole second marriage thing, but that can wait until the divorce papers are signed." She takes another sip of her water, and I have to fight back my laughter. The thought of her waiting is hilarious. She won't let the subject go. Not that she'll talk it to death; she'll do the complete opposite. This is where Rory gets her personality trait of holding it all in from, both of them thinking things to death. We'll let her keep thinking that she doesn't need the answer right away.

"If you wanna keep the girls in this house, I've got no problem selling mine, taking the equity from the sale of my place and building an addition. If you'd rather do that to my place, we can, too. Fuck, if you want to move completely, find a builder to get it done to our specifications, whatever it is, I'm game." I squeeze her leg, making sure she's got her eyes on mine, and proceed, "You'll have my ring on your finger, my last name attached to yours, and if the girls ever want or allow me to formally adopt them, I'll do that as well." I see the second Rosaleigh comprehends my words. Tears are creeping their way out of her eyes. I want so badly to wipe them away, and I could if I placed her in my lap.

"You have it all figured out. I should have known. You don't leave any stone left unturned. My God, it should have been you. Everyone around us knew it. I was the one late to the party, it seems." This time, my hands don't stay on her legs. I'm moving, sliding out of my chair, placing her feet on the floor, and I'm on my knees in front of her. She opens her thighs until I'm between them. My hands cup her cheeks, lips sliding along the seam of hers, coaxing her to open them. The tears streaming down aren't deterring me. Leigh's heard me tell her how I feel. Now I need to show her, starting with a kiss.

20

ROSALEIGH

I woke up this morning wound up like the Energizer bunny. How it didn't set alarm bells off for Rory and Emmy, I have no idea. Two days off in a row would usually have me happy, staying in bed until the last minute, luxuriating in the fact when I come back home, it's to hit the ground running. That isn't the case today. Nix kissed me good night last night after we talked. Our conversation was short, sweet, and to the point. Any question I had, he had an answer to. It was a balm to my soul the way he handles things. It also sucked because I was going to my bed, and he was going to his. I'd have thought sleep wouldn't come so easily, but the minute my head hit the pillow, I was out like a light, probably because there was nothing left unsettled. We knew where we stood and where things were going. Well, minus him giving me a complete answer on the having children with me front, a subject I'm sure to go over in my head multiple times an hour, a minute, it doesn't matter. I will think about it non-freaking-stop, wondering if I should get on birth control again or not. I was on it while married to David, only because he refused to get a vasectomy for so many years that I wanted to play it safe. It was only a couple of years ago that he finally made the appointment. After being on the pill for so long, I left it alone. It was only once he left and the bills piled up, when finding health insurance that was affordable for us three was out of the question. I found something decent for the girls, and I just pay cash in the event I need to see a doctor, which also means my birth control prescription has long since lapsed.

The thought of calling Ophelia is at the forefront of my mind. Too bad she's three hours behind me, and I've already called her enough in the past twenty-four hours to ask for advice, essentially bugging the shit out of her. Instead, after dropping the girls off at two different schools, so ready for them to finally get back to being together at the same school, at least for a year, if not two once they get older, I went to the grocery store, stocking up on what we'd need for the week. Then David's parents called asking if they could pick the girls up this afternoon and drop them off at our house. It was hard to say no; they truly are amazing grandparents. They didn't raise David to be the conniving dickhead he is; it just happened he turned out that way. Since Conrad and Sherry have the girls figured out, I came home to put away the groceries, grumbling over the fact that my girls are human garbage disposals. Keeping them fed and groceries in the house is nearly impossible. Then I cleaned the house from top to bottom, going so far as to even weed the flowerbeds to keep myself occupied until they come home.

Now, I've showered, washed my hair, and shaved my legs with no interruptions, not even so much as a phone call or a text from Rory, Emmy, Ya-Ya, Ophelia, and definitely not Phoenix. Not that I'm upset about the last person. Waking up to a good-morning text was all it took to make my day. It wasn't anything spectacular; it still doesn't stop me from pulling out my phone and reading that text from earlier.

> Nix: Good morning, sweetheart. I hope you have a good day.
>
> Me: Hey, good morning to you, too. Are you super busy today at the shop?
>
> Nix: Got a custom job coming in. I'll be home for dinner, if you and the girls want company.
>
> Me: You're always welcome here. I'm doing Italian grinder sandwiches, though, unless you're cooking?
>
> Nix: Sounds good to me. I'll cook tomorrow night, since you'll no doubt work until closing. I'll call if I get a break today. Tell the girls I said to have a good day. Love you.

I didn't respond, not because I didn't want to. It was time to get the show on the road in the form of drop-offs, then I was driving, so texting and being behind the wheel was a hard no. By the time I picked my phone back up, it seemed weird to text back hours later, so I left it alone, figuring the words spoken out loud to him would be better than through a text.

"Madre, we're home!" I'm still on my bed, flat on my

back, phone in my face, so lost in my own world I didn't even hear Sherry and Conrad pull into the driveway.

"In my room!" I holler back, unwilling to get up and greet them. Plus, there's nothing better than the girls piling in bed with me while we have a much-needed conversation.

"Mom, guess what?" Rory walks into my room, dropping her backpack to the floor, sliding out of the shoes I wore last night. Apparently, sweats, a shirt, and clogs were the style today. It was good to know the reason, too.

"Oh, I don't know. Did you talk to a new boy, or did you ace your test?" I sit up, scooching until my back is at the pillows, knowing I've got three seconds until she's jumping and wrapping her arms around me.

"I aced it. Boys are disgusting. I'm done with them. Aunt Fif and Nix gave me the scoop on how they're nothing but rodents at this age. I didn't miss a single freaking question!" Emmy is doing a dance, excited for her big sister, waiting her turn to talk to me about her day. We all know how important this test was for Rory.

"I'm so proud of you, baby girl." I squeeze her to my body, holding on for a bit longer. There will come a time when hugs won't happen a lot, and until that happens, I'm going to hold on a little longer.

"Thanks, Mom. Why are you in bed? You're never back here during the day," Rory asks.

"Yeah, Mamacita, what gives?" Emmy climbs in. Rory moves to one side to make room, and my arms wrap around both the girls, wondering how this is going to go and if it's going to bring more heartache.

"Well, that'd be because I got every chore and errand

done, then I got to relax. This having two days off in a row is like living a life of luxury." Easing them into the Phoenix-and-Mom talk is probably better than blabbing it out right away. That way, I can get a lay of the land.

"How was my Emmy's day?" I kiss the side of her head, then do the same to Rory, not leaving either one of them out.

"Fabulous, like always. You know, doing all the extra things for my teacher, taking attendance, walking kids up to the office while making it look fashionable." That's my Emmy, always proud of any accomplishment.

"I'm so proud of my girls. You two are taking the world by storm. There is a subject I'd like to talk to you about. One that the two of you have full control over if it happens or not." They both sit up, moving so they're facing me, which means they're no longer in my arms. That kind of stinks, but eye contact has always been our thing, too. The interest in their facial expressions has me on the edge of my seat, well, bed really, but that's hard to do when you're smack dab in the middle.

"Don't leave us hanging in suspense, Momsies!" Emmy says.

"Yeah, we need to know," Rory agrees.

"I want to know your opinion on me getting back into the dating world." I wince, not stating who it is I'd be dating until I know the answer.

"Oh my gosh! No way. Boys are gross. Look what that jerk wad did to my sister. I mean, unless it's a man like Nix, I don't think it's a good idea." I look at her. Shock is more than likely written all over my face. Clearly, he's made quite the impression on Emmy. I'm not surprised by that either, though, not really.

"Seriously, Nix is the shit, excuse my French, Mom." Rory rolls her eyes because she knows I'm the queen of cussing in the worst of times, sometimes even in the best when it's called for. I don't chide her about it often as long as it's used sparingly and not the worst of words. "He is, though, honestly, better than Dad ever was. Nix spends time with us, he helps us with homework, is always at our games or competitions, cooks like a world renown chef, and is an absolute smoke show. The girls at school go freaking stupid. I mean, he is handsome, but then there's that weird feeling because you know he's like the father we never had. Sorry, Emmy." That's a lot to say for the girl who usually thinks before she speaks, choosing carefully in case she inadvertently hurts feelings.

"No apology necessary. So, we can all agree. It's Phoenix or nothing, right? Right, good talk. Make it work, Mommalicious." She pats my hand like I'm a dog. That child of mine.

"Okay, so what if I told you that man I'm going to start dating is, in fact, no other than Nix?" I'm surrounded, literally. Both girls tackle me to the bed, happier than ever, singing Phoenix's praises, telling me they knew their mom had it but didn't know she *had* it. What *had* is, I have no idea. What I do know is that the James girls are on board and life couldn't get any freaking better.

"Yo, Eli, you got a minute?" I ask my lead mechanic. He's bent over the frame of an old beat-up Honda that's seen better days. The only thing the owner wants done is a service, says while it looks like a pile of shit, the car still runs like a dream. He wasn't totally right about that. The interior looks better than the exterior, I will say that. The body of the car is where the most damage is. Apparently, his son had no problem taking it out dogging the shit out of it.

"What's up, Nix?" Eli is older than me by a few years, been through some shit that made him one closed-off individual since the bitch who shall not be named raked him over the coals.

"You're divorce attorney, he any good?" His head is tipped to the side, knowing I'm not married. A slow smirk takes over his face, and I know I'm about to get a ration of hell. It doesn't matter that I'm the boss or the shop owner; everyone is treated like an equal individual.

"Fuck yeah. I'll send you his contact as soon as I'm finished for the day. He ain't cheap, though. Hope you got some cake to lay down for your lady." I've got more than enough sitting in my bank account. I'm not rich by any means, but the business does well for itself. Staying single for as long as I have has helped, too.

"I've got the money. Rosaleigh isn't going to let me help if she has any say about it. I'm not above going directly to the source if it means it won't knock out all of her savings," I tell him. When I called my parents today to tell them that Leigh and I were making shit official as long as the girls were cool with it, there was an *about fucking time* from my father, followed by an intake of breath, which I'm sure meant Mom whacked him in the stomach when he least expected it. Mom's response was more like '*Don't screw it up. Love that woman with your whole heart, take care of my girls, and you know Rory and Emmy are with you every step of the way.*' It felt good to know everyone was in our corner, even Ophelia, who's always giving me hell, told me to '*Go get her, tiger.*' The only worry I have now are the girls.

"He'll treat you well. She tried to go after my retirement, my house, and my cars after only six months of marriage. It could be that my situation was worse. She was fighting it at every turn, took what could be a simple signing of the papers with a wad of cash to get her out of my life to a drawn-out year-long affair. It was worth every fucking penny to see her walk away without a dime." He grabs a new toothpick off his toolbox, a habit he picked up when he quit smoking.

"I'm not sure a wanted felon can do a damn thing, and if he does,"—I shrug my shoulders—"well, we'll deal with that when it happens."

"It's a shit thing that fucker did to her. Everyone knows Rosaleigh is the shit, working more than anyone else at Minnie's, including the owner herself, how she'll drop off desserts at the nursing home, both of them when she has the time to back with her girls. Everyone in town knows the only thing the girl can make is sandwiches and cookies. You lucked out, brother. They're good people. That dumbass comes back into town, he won't have just you to deal with. Thinking the whole town will be out for blood." Eli isn't wrong about that. Leigh deserves the good life, to be able to live worry free, and judging by the text she sent me hours after the last one I sent her, all is good.

"Don't I know it, man. Thanks for the contact. Told Leigh I'd ask you, and knew if you used someone, she wouldn't be dicked around," I tell Eli, knowing how some people around here still have their judgments about Rosaleigh for what Douchebag David did, even though after the hell she was put through, everything turned out alright. I guess it was a good thing she demanded to have a joint checking account for the bills and separate for the rest. Douchebag David was pissed. He came to me like we were good friends at this point, telling me what Rosaleigh wanted after they'd gotten married. I listened to him bitch for nearly an hour, holding back my smile while doing so. There's a reason Leigh wanted that. My mother and I, we told her. It's better to be safe than sorry, to have something set aside for yourself in case shit went sideways. Rosaleigh took it to heart. It's what saved her in the long run, especially since the cops and feds froze David's account as well as their joint. If she hadn't had that cushion, it could have cost her the house, too, not that any of us would have let that happen. Leigh has her pride, though, and she'd rather move in with my parents than ever ask for a dollar.

"I get it. Speaking of, how's your sister doing? She still pissed at her boss?" I give him a look of complete bewilderment, having no idea that Eli talks to my sister. I sure as shit have no idea what he's talking about in regard to her boss.

"I talked to her this morning. She'll be here in a couple of weeks for Leigh's birthday. I've got no idea on the boss front. You wanna tell me what's going on?" I cross my arms over my chest, trying to gauge what he knows that I don't.

"Ophelia was here the last time she was in town, working on that nightmare of an office you've been dealing with ever since Sophie was fired for fucking up ordering parts, processing invoices, and all that other bullshit. We got to talking, and she mentioned her boss was a grade A dick, saying she was stuck in California for at least a little while longer because of some contract." Eli shrugs his shoulders. I lighten my stance. I'm not saying he's not a good guy. It's that his taste in women fucking sucks; at least it has in the past, even before his marriage to Lindsay. None of them were with Eli for Eli, after the money and the notoriety he had around town with the local motorcycle club.

"Son of a bitch. She hasn't said a word. I wonder if she told Rosaleigh. I'll have to ask her. If she's that miserable, surely there's a way out of the contract. As far as work, I'd hire her or Leigh in a minute. Fucking stubborn women won't hear any of that. I only get my sister in here when I play the I'm-screwed card, and in two weeks, when she's here, sees the state of the office, it'll be my balls she busts." There's a mountain of paperwork, more invoices than I know what to do with, calls I need to field and return. I need a new administrative assistant. The problem with that is, in our small town, there's no one I'm willing to bring on board after Sophie managed to mess up my whole computer system as well as everything else.

"You could see if Rory and Emmy want some spare money. They're smarter than Sophie ever was, and they could at least get the filing done and loaded into the new system," Eli suggests.

"That's not a bad idea. I'll have to run it by Leigh then see if the girls would be up for it." Rory would definitely want a job, considering the girl loves to shop, goes through more tubes of mascara than I ever thought humanly possible, and the only reason I know that little fact is while I'm giving her a ride to school, her eyes are glued to the visor mirror, coating on more shit than Fif ever did. I'm sure that's changed, and I know without a doubt where Rory got that from. Hell, last week, I was cleaning out my truck and found a handful of lip glosses and mascara tubes, all from Rory. How Leigh keeps up with her habit, I've got not one single clue.

"I'm more than a grease monkey." Eli taps his temple, leaving grease in its wake.

"Sure. You good to lock up? I'm done for the day," I ask him, ready to get home, grab a quick shower, and walk the few short steps it takes across the street to get to my girls.

"Yep, I won't be much longer. This Honda has about had all it's going to get. It's leaking radiator fluid like a stuck pig. So much for the man getting another couple of years out of it. Only so much a weld job will hold." Huh, didn't think it was that bad. Shows you what I know when I'm stuck in the fucking office unless I've got a customer who requests me by name. I went along with the Honda owner as he talked, looked under the hood, and it seemed alright to me. Eli knows his shit, though, and wouldn't fuck around a customer.

"I'll give him a call tomorrow if you want, deal with the fallout that might happen. Tell him what's going on and what his options are. He may get a few months out of it, but I don't want him sinking a pile of money into a pile of shit either."

"Sounds good. You talk to Ophelia, keep my name out of it. Something tells me she's got claws sharper than Lindsay, only in a different way." I nod. No fucking way am I getting into that or dealing with my sister potentially banging my employee. There are some things a brother does not want to fucking know, and that's one of them.

"Later." I'm already walking back to my office. The work can wait for another day. I've got more important people to surround myself with.

22

ROSALEIGH

"Are you guys sure you don't mind going to Ya-Ya's and Papou's for the night?" I ask the girls for probably the eighteenth time. They've been Team Nix and Mom all week long, making sure to be their normal selves, leaving us alone instead of barging in on our conversation at times.

"Yes, Mother. Real food, dessert, and shopping tomorrow. How could we ever mind?" Rory replies. Phoenix made the plans, wanting to take me out on a real date, asking his parents if they minded keeping the girls. He even offered to drop them off at their place. Ya-Ya was not having that. She said it was time she and Papou took them out to dinner and a movie. Which is why the girls are currently in the living room, bags packed, filled to the brim like they're going to be away for a week instead of a night and half the day tomorrow. My girls are a trip, and if they think I didn't notice Nix slipping them a few gift cards last night, they're sorely mistaken. A talk that will be happening tonight when it's just the two of us. If he's going to give them extras, my girls need to pull their weight and help him in some kind of way.

"Yeah, like, how could we not go? It's been soooo long since we've stayed with them." Emmy throws her body onto the couch, landing on my lap. This dramatic child of mine, and she's only ten. By the time she's Rory's age, I'm going to need to have the patience of a saint knowing that the theatrics will become next level.

"Good, now here's the hard talk. I know Nix gave you gift cards, and I know you have the cash you've earned. We all know Ya-Ya is going to spoil you. I only ask that you don't take advantage. Anything extra you want, you pay for. And be prepared; you'll be figuring out how to help Nix out around his house for him keeping you flush with funds." I play with the ends of Emmy's hair while looking at Rory, silently asking her to keep her eye on Emmy.

"We will, promise, Mom." This comes from my oldest daughter, who's sitting in the oversized chair, wearing clothes that came out of my closet, courtesy of Ophelia. There were a lot of clothes that there was no way I'd get the chance to wear, so it became this communal closet the girls could use when they felt the need. Especially Rory when she wasn't wearing sweats. Emmy couldn't be bothered. What I did notice is that she's been wearing the shirt Nix gave her to bed, the one that has his shop name emblazoned on the front, oversized in its style, which doesn't deter Emmy in the least.

"Fine, I won't ask for two new pairs of Chucks. I'll only ask for one." I lay my head back, closing my eyes. Lord, give me strength for my second child, the one who gives zero fucks about what people think about her, the carefree one, the one with an independent streak a mile wide, the one where it's a slippery slope on how not to staunch the spreading of her wings.

"That'd be much appreciated. It's nice for them to take you out and to offer to buy you things. It's rude for you to take advantage of them, right?" Emmy lifts her body off my lap. Unsure of what she's up to next, I brace for whatever comes my way.

"I know, Madre. Have fun with Nix. Don't worry about us. You two go have a night out. Rory will tattle if I do something wrong." Our week has been jam-packed with work, school, home, to either me cooking or Nix cooking, him staying until I'm yawning so much that it sucks when he has to say good-bye. What it did give us was time to connect as a couple instead of friends, not to mention the way the man kisses. Oh my God, he is freaking incredible. His lips and mouth take any worry away that I could possibly have, not to mention the quiet orgasms he's given me. It sucked because he has yet to let me reciprocate, an action that I won't be denied tonight. That's another thing—my hours at the nursery this week have literally been a dream. I'm not sure if it's all the overtime I worked while everyone was sick or what. All I know is that when I got my schedule on Tuesday, it gave me hours that worked with the girls' schedule—nine o'clock in the morning was clock-in time, and five o'clock in the evening was quitting time. And get this, I have Saturday and Sunday off this weekend. I am not rocking that boat because as soon as I ask, the following week will be an absolute shit show.

"That's Ya-Ya and Papou. Love you!" Rory stands up, picks up her bag, tosses it over her shoulder, and walks toward me so I can at least say my goodbyes.

"I love you. Be good, be respectful, and text me before you go to bed." I stand up, hugging Rory while Emmy scrambles to get to her bag. They might be telling me their goodbyes now; that doesn't mean I won't be walking them out the door and greeting the people who I adore more than ever, the two people who took in a young girl who only wanted to know what it felt like to be loved by a family.

"Love you. Now come see us off, but don't take too long. We have things to do, people to see, and you have a date to get ready for." Emmy loops her arm around mine as we walk out of the house, take the step down, and walk to the driveway. Ya-Ya doesn't get out of the car; neither does Papou. I'm not upset in the least; they're giving me a massive gift tonight.

"Come give me a smooch," Papou states. I dip my head, kissing him on the cheek.

"Thank you," I tell him. He takes my hand in his. The girls are too busy saying hello to Ya-Ya to hear us.

"No, thank you, sweet Rosaleigh. Never seen my boy happier. Never seen you girls that way either. You both have a good night, and don't worry about us. Ya-Ya has a lot planned for tomorrow. She'll call you when we're on our way, but don't expect us back till after dinner." I'm at a loss for words, not that I should be surprised. Rory and Emmy are their only grandkids. It didn't matter if they were blood or not, we were all theirs.

"Alright, don't spend all your money on them." He goes to argue, but I just keep talking, "They have money, some they earned, some they didn't. I know you love them, but you two hanging out with them is all they really need."

"Tell that to Ya-Ya. Now get out of here. We've got dinner and a show booked. Have fun, Leigh." I look through the window. Both girls are buckled in the backseat of their car, and Ya-Ya has a smile a mile wide plastered across her face.

"Go, have fun. We'll chat later. Love you, Rosaleigh," Ya-Ya says. I barely nod my agreement before they're backing out of the driveway, Emmy waving goodbye out the open window, and I stand there until the only thing I can see are the taillights in the distance. I start to head back inside, feeling a ton of weight lifted off my shoulders. The girls with their grandparents, either side, really, I know they're in safe hands. That's why instead of heading back inside to get ready for my date with Nix, I'm doing something else entirely. There's only one place I want to be, and that's in the arms of the man who has teased me relentlessly all week. My feet carry me to Phoenix's house, walking up the steps, a pep in my step, knowing I'm going to throw a wrench in his plans the minute he opens the door.

23

NIX

"Jesus Christ." The beating on the door doesn't stop. I was in the shower, working my cock. That way, I'm not coming with the first thrust inside of Rosaleigh. That all ended when the doorbell wouldn't quit ringing, only for the banging on the door to start. At first, I thought it might be Emmy or Rory, but I knew that wasn't the case before I stepped in the shower. Rory sent me a text saying they were gone and was thanking me once again for the gift cards I gave them.

"Phoenix." Rosaleigh is standing in front of me when I open the door, a towel wrapped around my waist. She's in another one of her tank tops, nothing beneath it judging by her pebbled nipples, and when she licks her lips, the only thing I can do is pull her inside my house before we give the neighbors a show they'd never forget.

"Leigh." My hands fist her hair as my body walks her back, the towel loosening from my strides but also

Rosaleigh's hands that pull at the material. A moan is pulled from her when her palm wraps around my shaft. Clearly, she's tired of waiting. This week has been a lesson in patience more for me than for Leigh. While I've made sure she's gotten hers, any time she's attempted to use her hand or her mouth on my body, I've backed away. I could quite her moans with my own. If she were to suck my cock, there would be no way I'd be able to keep my mouth shut, instructing her on how I want her to suck me, to scrape her teeth along my shaft, to roll my balls in the palm of her hands.

"I'm tired of waiting, Nix, please." She breaks away from my mouth, pleading with me to give her what we both want. Had I known this is what she was after, I would have at least stripped her of the clothes she's wearing. As it is. it'll take a few extra minutes to make it to my bedroom while I strip her of the clothes that are hiding her amazing fucking body, to see her spread out on my sheets, and to commit it to memory while doing so. Fuck yeah.

"Not going to, but not here, against the door, the first time. I'm going to take my time, wrench every drop of pleasure from your body." Her body gives away her desire; the red undertone of her skin blooms like the prettiest blush.

"I'm not opposed to come back to sex against the door. It can be one of my firsts." That motherfucker. I knew he was selfless callous dick, but not that much of one.

"We're not talking about the past today. We'll come back to that. I'm going to take you everywhere, Leigh—against the door, in the shower, spread out on my table while I eat you, on the hood of my car, fucking everywhere." I'd like to say

I'm not rushing to get her into my room, but I am. The need to have her bare, my cock tunneling in and out of her tight, wet heat. That's why instead of pulling her around with her hand clasped in mine, I'm sliding her shorts down with both hands, pulling at the material at her lower back. Leigh shifts her legs until they drop to the floor. I'm lucking out that she isn't wearing panties either. My fucking day has been made a million times over. I grip the edge of her shirt, taking it off her so we're both naked, and then I'm grabbing her hips, lifting her off the ground. "Wrap your legs around me, sweetheart." Her hands slide from my shoulders until they're cupping the back of my neck, eyes full of delight now that my cock is pressed against her wet slit.

"Hurry, please." With every step, the underside of my cock hits her clit. Leigh's body moves of its own accord, reaching for that orgasm she's desperate for. I almost veer us to the couch. If it weren't for the need to see her in my bed, my scent lingering on her skin, while I paint the depths of her pussy with my cum, I would.

"A few mores steps, Leigh. You keep using my body as your personal playground, foreplay won't be happening, not once were in my bedroom. You want to suck my cock, it'll have to wait. You want my head between your thighs, we'll make it work so it happens at the same time," I grunt out when she lifts her body. The tips of my fingers dig into her soft flesh when I feel the head of my cock being sucked inside Rosaleigh's cunt. The sex kitten has come out to play. It's on the tip of my tongue to tell her to slow down. I can't, though, not when she's this wild and carefree. What I do is make my way into my bedroom faster, quickening my steps.

"God, you're huge." She tries to slide down further, but I hold her off, seeing the bed in my line of sight.

"Hold off. Not even a minute left, and you'll feel how big I am when I'm taking you. It's going to start with you on your back, your legs on top of my shoulders. I need to watch your face as you fall apart. The second go-around, it's your choice. How do you want it, Rosaleigh?" The husk in my voice must do something to her; it's that or telling her exactly what I'm going to do to her delicious body. She should be used to my mouth by now. Every night this week, I've told her in vivid detail how it's going to be once we finally get some free time.

"I want to ride you, doing the work, feeling the burn in my body as I work you over like I know you'll be doing soon enough." I keep my cock notched at the entrance of her pussy, the head being swallowed by her wet depths as I lay her down on my unmade bed. Rosaleigh's blonde waves fan around her. Her tits are full, ripe for my hands, knowing she used them to feed the girls after carrying them in her body for nine months. There's no way my cum won't be inside her multiple times throughout the night, since us going out on a date isn't going to happen. We'll order dinner in, or I'll cook. Whatever we do, it'll involve us staying naked.

"Anything you want, it's yours," I tell her. My hands cup her tits, thumbs gliding over her pebbled nipples, mouth salivating. I'm not sure where to start—her mouth, the underside her ear that I know causes her cunt to clench in need, her neck, or to take her nipples one at a time, latching on to one, sucking deeply until she's writhing, head shaking, trying to run away from the dual sensation when I'm fucking her with my fingers while working her tits.

"Right now, I want you to finally take me. I want to be yours as much as you're mine." There's no more holding back. I slide in another inch, worried that if I slam deep inside her, like my body is begging for me to do, I'll cause her pain.

"I'm going to. Fuck, Leigh, you're so tight, strangling my cock." She's already in the throes of rapture. I move one of my hands away from her tit, sliding down the middle of her abdomen, watching her the entire time, the way she sucks in a breath, body begging me to continue touching her. My thumb sweeps across her bare pussy as I push in further until I'm half inside her before I pull back a bit, gathering the wetness that's coating my dick with my thumb, so I can use it while I manipulate her clit to where she's making the sweetest noises possible. A cross between a moan and a whimper.

"More, Nix, more. You feel so good." Her legs are wrapped around my waist, and she pulls me closer with her feet at the small of my back. I should have held strong, not allowed her the movement. Clearly, I wasn't strong enough, and we both need one another. I'm slammed in to the hilt, looking down at the way her pussy is holding my cock firmly in its place, not moving until the quivers of her center slow down. It's one thing to come prematurely; it's another when you can't even get your woman there before you lose it, and that's something I'm not going to let happen.

"You good, sweetheart?" I ask, plucking her nipple with my thumb and pointer finger, thumb still sliding over her clit, moving it in a circular motion all while staying still until she adjusts to my length inside her.

"Even my biggest toy doesn't compare to you," she admits. I smirk, remembering seeing the drawer full of toys and thinking the same exact thing. It almost had me getting on a website or driving to another town to pick up one more my size. There wasn't enough time during the week, and I know for a fact I'd be the one wanting to use it on her the first time.

"I warned you. I'm going to start moving now. Place your legs on my shoulders." Her eyes flash with desire. It's been a long-as-fuck time for her, but it's been twice as long for me.

"Okay." I move my hands away from her body, annoyed because it means letting go, and that's the last damn thing I ever want to do when it comes to Rosaleigh. As soon as she's situated, my hands grip her hips, pressing her further into the mattress as I climb on top, the front of my thighs touching the back of hers, knees giving me leverage, and then I'm working my cock. There's no going slow any longer. If she's hurting tomorrow, then I guess I'll be the one to draw her a tub full of hot water, bring her aspirin, and fuck her with my mouth until she's ready for me to take her again.

"Fuck," I groan. The wet velvet clench of Leigh's pussy lures me in, making me shudder. The only noises are our heavy breathing. My eyes are focused on hers, reading her thoughts, seeing that she's ready for me to let go, to quit holding back. It seems my woman wants me to claim her. It's a damn good thing, too, because while I was using her bathroom the other night, I did some searching. Not a single sign of birth control pills was in sight, not in the bathroom, not in her nightstand, and not in any drawers in her dresser. I'd have seen them in the kitchen with all the times I've cooked, so I knew none were there. Plus, with the girls around, I'm sure Leigh would keep them out of sight.

"Holy shit." The breath leaves me as I watch her eyes roll to the back of her head, like she was in the process of rolling them, only the lids are now closed. I don't admonish her for not keeping her eyes on me. Even if I wanted that, it's hard to ignore how her body quivers with every push of my hips, pulling back only to slide back inside. Rosaleigh's pretty pussy has a stranglehold on me, and I fucking love it. My eyes move from her face, to the the deep crimson blush coating her chest, her cherry-tipped nipples that I've tasted as many times as I possibly could this week, knowing how they feel when I'm sucking them into my mouth, cheeks hollowing out with every pull. The fact that Leigh likes a little pain with her pleasure only makes it that much more enjoyable. I watch as her tits move up and down with every shove inside her. It only adds to the beauty. My eyes move to her stomach, knowing one day soon, she'll be carrying my child in her belly. This time, it'll be me there to hold her hair as she goes through bouts of morning sickness. I'll be the one who takes care of her aches and pains, the influx of hormones. Fuck yeah, that'll all be taken care of by me. In fact, I move my hand that was on her hip, not needing it for leverage any longer, and place it on her lower abdomen, imagining the life that is sure to take hold on this very night. Her eyes open. No words are spoken, only our moans can be heard through the bedroom. Rosaleigh's legs tighten around my neck. I watch as the lips of her pussy flutter along the length of my dick. She's about to come, and she's about to take me with her.

"Nix, God, Nix." I move so her legs are off my shoulders, pressing my body to hers while maintaining my momentum, wanting to propel her into the orgasm she's so close to reaching. The nerves along my back constrict, and my hands delve into her hair. We're face to face. Every breath she takes I breathe in; it goes both ways. This time when her neck arches, I don't do a damn thing to deter her, wanting to watch the emotions flood her face.

"That's it, sweetheart, let go and take me with you," I grunt as my own orgasm starts to take over my body. I slam inside her one last time. The cum jetting from my cock bathes her pussy, and I stay right where I am as I empty inside the woman who was always meant to be mine.

Rosaleigh doesn't move either, not even when I reposition us, so her legs are up higher on my back. I read in a magazine somewhere that if a woman keeps them up long enough, it'll help get her pregnant. I've got one forearm to the bed, my other hand playing with the strands of her hair as she takes her time to open her eyes for me. The fact that I could stay like this, live in her sweet-as-fuck heat forever doesn't bother me. It'd be a fuck of a way to start and end my days.

"I think my legs are broken. Isn't that how the saying goes? If a woman can make you a sandwich after sex, you didn't do the job right? Well, I can assure you, there will be no food making of any kind. In fact, you'll have to be the one to bring food to me because I am broken in the most amazing way possible." Leigh's eyes open. She's got a smile on her face, and if she hasn't realized I've come inside her yet, she will soon. I'm only hoping it doesn't backfire on me.

The conversation was left pretty open ended on both of our parts.

"No walking required on your part. I will say our date night out is becoming a date night in. You've got your choice of dinner, though. Either I can cook, or we can order from the diner and have it delivered." Her stomach takes that time to rumble its hunger.

"Diner. Cheeseburger wrap, extra pickles, no onions, and seasoned fries. Oh, and medium-rare on the burger, please." I guess that answers my question.

"As if I didn't know that already. I've got Diet Coke in the fridge for you. I know the diner only carries Pepsi products." She scrunches her nose at the thought of drinking Diet Pepsi.

"Thank you. I'd get up, but I'm currently comfortable. Even if there's a strong man lying on top of me." My cock gives its nod of approval by flexing inside of her cunt.

"Anytime. I'm not going anywhere just yet." I've got at least a few more minutes until the magazine said it'd be safe to pull out.

"Good, because I like you right where you are." Her hands goes to the back of my head, pulling me closer until our lips meet. I give in to whatever she wants as long as I can stay right here with her.

24

ROSALEIGH

I wake up warm. A body is lying half on me, half off, and a hand is cupping me between my legs, which is exactly how I fell asleep. Phoenix tried to be a gentleman by keeping his cock out of me. I wasn't having that. I might be sore in a way that leaves me feeling his presence throughout the day, but that's not considered a bad thing in my book.

"Go back to sleep. I can hear your brain thinking already. We've got an hour before we need to start getting ready for the day, and, woman, you've worn me out." Nix may act like he's tired. Tell that to his finger that is now working its way in and out of my pussy. I'd say he's not worn out at all.

"Are you saying three times is all you're up for?" I don't bother with asking about where we're going in an hour from now. Maybe Nix is going somewhere, but I'm staying in his bed all day until it's time to go home because the girls are back.

"Oh, I've got more in me. That doesn't mean I'm willing to get out of bed just yet, or move. I like you right where you are." My center is slick with wetness; his fingers are coated in it. The lazy ebb and flow Nix is creating doesn't help me quench my desire in the least for someone who is claiming to be worn out, and that person is definitely not me. Since Nix and I started this thing, I've found a new lease on life, happy for the first time in years save my daughters. Those girls are always brightening my world, even on the darkest days.

"What do you mean we have an hour, Nix? The girls won't be home for awhile. All I want to do is stay in bed." Last night, true to his words, dinner was delivered. I stayed in bed, only slipping on a tee shirt I found on the dresser. It was folded, smelt like Nix, and now it's mine, or it was until I was divested of said shirt after dinner, and he pulled me on his lap, lining his cock up to my center, and I sank down slowly.

"The girls texted the group chat this morning." Emmy set that up Monday night while we were all together in the kitchen, Nix and I working together to make the Italian grinder sandwiches. Of course, his contribution was making homemade potato chips. Who even knew that was a thing? This is why, for the rest of the week, Emmy and Rory would shoot off texts in the group making requests for what they'd like for dinner. I only smiled and laughed after reading them on my lunch break or after work. There's really no competition when it comes to my cooking versus Nix's—he wins hands down.

"Oh yeah? What catastrophe happened now?" I roll over

so we're face to face, throwing my leg over his hip. Phoenix still has his fingers inside of me. Now I kind of hope he takes them out and uses his cock instead.

"Apparently, after dinner and the show last night, they did some shopping. Now they're eating breakfast, then shop again. Jesus, how my dad corralled them all this long is amazing. Anyways, the girls want to come home after lunch." I moan when his thumb presses against my clit. I try to keep my eyes open but fail epically. He works me up at a steady pace. If he'd go a bit faster, I'd be coming like lightning.

"I guess that means our day of luxuriating in your bed is coming to an end. I love my girls, so I'm going with Ya-Ya shopped them till they dropped, and now they're ready to be bumps on a log. Oh God. Right there." I arch my back. Nix doesn't take the bait, much to my chagrin. What does a girl have to do to get an orgasm from her man?

"Not yet. I'm going to keep fucking you with my fingers. The next thing I'm about to tell you today may piss you off. Before I tell you what we're doing, I'll tell you this. I'm going to be in your corner. Your schedule isn't allowing for this to happen during the week, so while yes, I pulled some strings, asked for a favor, I did it for you." He flicks his fingers back and forth inside me, getting what he wants, me not to be upset because I'm pretty sure if Nix is leading up to it this way, it's sure to piss me off.

"If you stop, I'm going to walk home butt naked, pull out a toy, and use it my damn self." This foreplay session has gone on entirely too long. I'm ready to either get off with his fingers or take it into my own hands, literally. It doesn't matter, but this teetering on the edge is pure torture.

"We've got an appointment with a divorce attorney in an hour. Eli recommended him. He's not cheap, but he's not too expensive either. I'm paying for the consult since I'm fucking determined to have you out of that douchebag's name. Consider it my early birthday present mixed with yours." My eyes snap wide, jaw hanging open, and I'm ready to light a fire under Phoenix Drakos' ass. I did the research on what the going rates were. They were not cheap. The good news was most used your consult fee and put it toward your retainer if you went with them, which is why I wanted to find the perfect fit.

"Nix, you did not." Phoenix doubles down, thumb to my clit, working in smooth circles, his fingers sliding back and forth in a fevered pace, all while doing something with the two digits inside me, a seesaw-like effect that has me bearing down.

"Fuck yeah, I like that look on your face, sweetheart. Take my fingers. Fuck your pussy on them and come for me." I let out a long moan, deep and throaty. Nix with his dirty mouth and the dirtier things he does to my body. My orgasm is long, drawn out. I'm completely and totally sated. I should still be upset with him for overstepping his bounds. It should have been me who made the appointment and spent the money.

"Come on. Time for a shower, coffee, and a small snack. You can yell at me later." He slides his fingers out of my center, dragging the tips up to the middle of my chest. The scent of our lovemaking bathes our bodies. Right now, though, it's my unique aroma that has me thinking of having Nix in another way. He doesn't allow that, not if we have an appointment to get to.

"Don't you dare. You know what that does to me," I admonish him. That doesn't deter him. Just when I think he's going to paint my lips with my wetness, he does the complete opposite, wrecking my world even more. He slides his fingers into his mouth, licking them clean.

"We're going to this appointment, getting the ball rolling, then we're grabbing lunch. By the time we're done, the girls will be home. What I will be doing is sleeping in your bed tonight and every night from here on out. If the girls aren't home, we'll stay here. Two nights I've had you in my arms; not liking when it doesn't happen."

"I should be pissed at you. I only asked if you knew of an attorney. Had I known you would go around me to get this set up, I wouldn't have asked. On the other hand, this is pure Nix. Once you made me yours, I became yours in every sense of the words. As for the girls, you're on your own asking that," I tease. It won't matter if I put my foot down and said no to the girls. They'd side with Nix and tell me to get with the twenty-first century. I can see Emmy stomping her foot, hands wrapped across her chest and throwing her sassy attitude. Rory would roll her eyes, go to my bedroom, clear out a drawer for Nix, and then walk away.

"I've got no problem with talking to the girls. I knew you'd be upset, Leigh, but that wasn't stopping me. It's the closure you all need. You can't erase the past, but you can change the future." There are no words for me to say. Nix is right, and that's why I tackle him until he's on his back. My

lips attack his, kissing him with everything I'm feeling—
hopefulness, happiness, all the things I can't put into words
go into our kiss. It doesn't take long for him to take over,
dominating my mouth with his, and then I'm sliding my
body down. His cock is hard and heavy between the two of
us. I want to thank him in the best possible way. I lift my
body slightly and then lower myself down. We don't last
long, both caught up in the moment of chasing our orgasms
together, not pulling away from one another until it's several
minutes later, even then it's hard to find the energy to leave
the bed. The only thing that gets me moving is that I'll be
damned if I allow Nix to lose the money for the attorney.
Plus, he's right. I'm ready to close the door on the past and
open a new one for the future.

25

ROSALEIGH

Two Weeks Later

"I CAN'T BELIEVE you're here, and for the whole freaking weekend," I tell my best friend. We're at a restaurant, only the two of us. Nothing but time on our hands. I'm drinking a glass of red wine. Ophelia doing the same, only hers is white and fruity whereas I'm more a dry kind of wine drinker. In my early twenties, I was all about the sweet concoctions. That's not the case these past few years. The way a good Cabernet Sauvignon or a Pinot Noir settles deep in your stomach, giving you that warm sensation, is what I like most.

"I've never missed your birthday. I wasn't going to start now. Plus, Phoenix paid my way out here this time around. Speaking of. Spill the freaking beans. I love my brother, but he's a tight-lipped virgin when the topic includes your relationship." I opened the door to Ophelia this afternoon, completely unexpected and surprised. The girls are still at school, and Nix is still at work, so we decided to take a car to the restaurant, knowing in order to hire an Uber in our small town, you had to do it early, and head home at a decent hour, too.

"Well, we're both all in. The girls are all in. Honestly, they'd probably choose your brother over me any day of the week. He listens, he talks, he helps out when I'm stuck at work, he kicks ass in math, so Rory, who has always struggled, is excelling. He and Emmy work on the car or at the shop during their spare time. Your brother is, well, he's perfect." I don't tell her we've whispered those three words aloud to one another, that he's at my place more than he's at his own, how he's made it clear it won't be happening much longer. The girls know he's permanent, I know he's permanent, so we only have to figure out if we're going to stay in my house, his house, or look for a new house.

"Oh, gag me. There's no way he's perfect. I grew up with him, remember. You did as well. How can you forget how he'd leave his stinky socks in the living room or how he'd burp as loudly as he could when the parents weren't around?" I roll my eyes, take another sip of my wine as we wait for our dinner to arrive. Ophelia and I already polished off one glass of wine each. We're working on our second, along with the fresh bread and butter. We practically inhaled it, lathering it with butter, hardly talking, too busy filling our mouths with the warm, chewy goodness.

"I remember. He's also in his thirties and a man who's

been on his own for a really long time." I'm not an idiot. There was a reason Nix chose to stay single all these years, never bringing anyone around the girls whom he may have dated. At first, I thought it was what he preferred. The small tidbits of information he's let on told me otherwise.

"Fine, fine. Want another glass of wine?" she asks, changing the subject, which is good because I'm ready to turn the focus back to her. Ophelia with the honey brown hair, same blue eyes as her brother; it's the dark circles under those eyes that I'm having a hard time ignoring. Not only that, she's skinnier than the last time I saw her.

"Sure." The money I saved up for the attorney was more than enough by half, two grand out the door when it's all said and done. With David being missing in action, he said it's a cut-and-dry case, what with the warrants out for his arrest. The likelihood for him coming around is slim to none. If he were incarcerated, it'd still be the same way. I took the other three thousand and paid off my Tahoe. No more five-hundred-dollar-a-month car payment meant that I could splurge on my birthday dinner.

"So, you know one of the things Nix and I talked about was what we'd do to either of our houses once he moved in or vice versa. That means one of them will be empty," I lead in, trying to talk it up. Ophelia made a mistake a lot of young people make, going to a college for a degree because you thought that was what you were supposed to do. I mean, she did stay in town at the local college, so her debt was minimal, but when she realized fashion design school was calling Fif's name, that meant moving from our small town across country, racking up a pile of student debt, and staying in

California for an eternity, unless she's at a different location for a movie or television show. "If you want first dibs before we decide if we'll rent or sell, it's yours." I did not clear this with the man I love, already knowing he'd be happy to have his younger sister back home.

"Is this going to be soon, like in the next few months, or longer down the road?" At least this time, she's not shooting me down right away like the last time.

"We'll make it work for however long you need. If that means a short-term rental until you're ready to come back home, that's what we'll do, okay?" I want my best friend home. Sure, there are some selfish reasons involved, but for the most part, it's the way Ophelia currently looks like a shell of herself. I can relate. It wasn't long ago that I was her, when I looked in the mirror and saw my hair thinning from stress, my body skinnier than ever from not eating a balanced diet, living off caffeine in the form of coffee and Diet Coke. Except, instead of dark circles like Ophelia is sporting, I had bags under my eyes so big they could pack a suitcase.

"I'm going to take that into consideration. I have an exit plan, you know?" I nod, wanting her to keep going as the waiter delivers our food and pours another glass of wine for each of us. I ordered the spicy shrimp tacos with a side of fries. Ophelia got her usual chicken tenders and French fries. It doesn't matter where we go, this is what she orders if her mom or Nix isn't cooking. "One more year. It was two years, but no way can I hold on that long. People think New York doesn't sleep, but California is ten times worse when it comes to celebrities and their executives. Anyways, by that time, I'll be completely debt free, and if I make the move too soon, I'll lose the clientele I've been slowly working for on the side. It's a double-edged sword, one that I'm having a hard time separating. God, coming home sounds amazing. I'll have to travel, which is still one of my favorite things to do, but it'll be once a month versus every other day." She takes a break from talking, going after a chicken tender. I do the same, except I'm devouring my tacos. The spice is on point and burning my mouth in the most decadent way. I grab my glass of wine, knowing a third will be in my near future, and then I'll really be tipsy.

"Oh God, these are the best," I tell her after I chew my food. "Then it's settled. You'll have a place to land when you're ready. Now, are you coming back to the house with me, or do you have other plans?" I don't ask for any other details about her work life, wanting her to truly be on vacation while she's home. Plus, Fif is the person who if you pry too much too soon, she'll close up like a clam.

"I'm hanging with Eli tonight. I'll be back over tomorrow for breakfast." I wiggle my eyebrows. Ophelia is playing with fire. Eli is pushing forty, not that age is anything except a number. He's also Nix's employee, went through a messy divorce and came out on top. I know my man, though. He's not going to take this sitting down, not when it comes to protecting the women in his life.

"I'm going to need another glass of wine. You call for an Uber, I'll call Nix for a ride." Only I'm not thinking about a ride in a vehicle. The girls are at David's parents' tonight, though they made it a stipulation to be home for breakfast since Nix was going all out for my birthday that isn't until tomorrow.

"Oh God, I know that look. Do not say it. Do not even go there." I snort. We continue eating and drinking until we're full and I'm tipsy. Ophelia is the one who ends up calling Nix once we're done with our dinner, the wine taking ahold of my body, going from tipsy to damn near drunk, and I can't wait to have drunken sex for the first time ever.

26

NIX

"She's all yours, big brother." Ophelia meets me outside the restaurant with Rosaleigh standing beside her, well, more like Leigh has her head resting on my sister's shoulder, a happy drunken smile permanently etched on her face as I get out of my truck to walk around.

"I see how it is. You get my woman smashed, then I'm left to pick up the pieces." Not that I mind. The words, *wined, dined, and sixty-nined* almost came out of my mouth. They probably would have if she weren't my sister.

"I'm right here, you two." Leigh moves from her place by Ophelia, walking as normal as she can. My hands go to her hips as soon as she's in reaching distance to steady her sway.

"Do you need a ride, Fif?" I ask over Rosaleigh's shoulder, ready to get my woman home. She's a lot of fun without having any alcohol in her system. I'm imagining she'll be twice as amazing, with no inhibitions. The girls aren't home, so we don't have to worry about either one of them barging into the bedroom. I won't say it's put a damper on our sex life, but it has made us have to shake things up and get creative.

"Nope, I'll see you tomorrow bright and early. I'll bring mimosas and Bloody Marys. Something tells me Leigh-Leigh is going to need the hair of the dog." That's the last thing Rosaleigh will need, but I won't tell her that. I'm positive that will all be for my sister.

"Alright, as long as you're sure?" I ask again, reluctant to leave her out here by herself.

"I'm sure. My Uber just arrived. Take your woman home. She's got stars in her eyes. My best friend might not have admitted it out loud before, so I'll tell you the truth. She's loved you for a long time, even when she was too young for you or David. He was more cunning than you. You wanted to give her the world, let her live her life. David always was a conceited asshole. That's why you're the man standing where you are, beside a woman who loves you more than anything. I'm happy for you." Leigh's forehead is pressed to my chest. Ophelia might think she's out of it, but judging by the deep breath, she heard it all.

"I still haven't had that conversation. It's coming soon, too. Love you, sis. See you tomorrow."

"Good, she deserves to know you were saving her." She walks away, heading to her hired car. I don't say anything, only making sure my sister gets in the car safe and sound, then I pick Leigh up by the hips, figuring carrying her to the passenger side of the truck isn't a bad idea. The minute she wraps those sexy-as-fuck legs around my waist, I slide my hand down to her ass, making sure she's not giving people a view in the dress she's wearing. That's for my eyes and my eyes only.

"Come on, sweetheart, let's get you horizontal." Her lips graze my throat, sucking the skin into her mouth, and I let her. Even when the door is open, her ass placed on the seat, I stand there, letting her mark me. It's only fair since I've been doing the same thing. While she's sucking me deep into her throat, I'd pull her off before I was coming in her mouth, picking her up and slamming inside her cunt, feeling the rippling her flesh surrounding my length and holding myself there as her body pulls my cum from me.

"I love you, Nix. I heard everything Fif had to say, and we'll talk about that later. Right now, I really want to mark one of those things off my *Never Have I Ever* list." She pulls away from the crook of my neck. I look at the teasing temptation that is Rosaleigh—eyes glazed, coy smile in place, tits moving with every breath she takes as my eyes move down the length of her body. The way her legs are spread, the skirt of her dress is above her hips. My tongue moistens my lower lip at seeing that she's drenched, soaking through her panties.

"I love you, too. What's the question, sweetheart?" I stay where I am, hands on top of her thighs, holding them there when it's the last thing I want to do.

"Actually, it's two. Drunk sex and sex in a car. Can I ask for that to be my birthday present this year? I mean, you've done a lot for me already, so if you say no, well, that's okay, too." She's talking about how I made the appointment for the attorney. How she was able to save money, that I told her to pay a bill off with. If it was credit cards, pay off the lowest one, doing the snowball effect. Leigh didn't have that. The only thing she had a note out in her name was the house and her Tahoe, which is now paid off. I barely did anything with the divorce but put a good chunk down on the consult fee to go toward her retainer. I'm keeping that between me and Mr. McCallister. Leigh's eyes drop to her lap, watching as my thumbs slide along the inside of her thighs.

"Anything you want, it's yours, especially that. Slide in, sweetheart. I can't take you here when anyone could come out and watch me fuck you until you come. I can take you down the road. We'll have the view of the water, the moon hanging above us, and you sitting on my cock." I move so my thumb is against her clit. I'm thinking about sliding her panties to the side and getting it wet before bringing it to my mouth, a move Leigh loves. "Slide in. I've got a woman to please." I step back, pull my shirt over my jeans to hide my cock that is making its presence known. Rosaleigh scoots back, swinging her legs as she does, not moving her dress down, and I know exactly where my hand will be as I drive down the road. "Seatbelt," I grunt before I close the door and walk around the front of the truck hoping like hell she isn't so drunk she'll fall asleep on me before we finish the short five-minute drive to where I know we won't have an audience. Since I left my truck running, I jump inside, put my own belt in place, foot on the brake, slam the vehicle in drive, and head to our destination.

"You okay, Leigh?" I ask, my hand moving directly to the apex of her thighs. Her legs fall open. Meanwhile, I'm having a hard time maintaining my focus, feeling the wetness seeping from her panties. I hook my finger to the side of the delicate lace, hitting smooth bare skin and sweet silky wetness. I'm coasting along the highway. The truck is silent, minus our breathing, hers because I know my woman. She's close to coming. Two more turns, and all I'll have to do is park the truck, lift her up, rip the flimsy excuse of panties off her body, undo my jeans, and then slide inside of Rosaleigh.

"I'd be better if your cock were inside me." I push down on the gas, taking the last turn a little too fast, kicking up the dirt, finding the area vacant like I knew I would. God bless small towns.

"One more minute. Take your panties off, and then your seatbelt." I park in a secluded area, trees covering the truck deep in an alcove, sand beneath the tires from the river front. I whip my seatbelt off, hit the lever on my seat, pushing it back until it's as far as it can go.

"They're already off." My eyes catch hers. She's completely bare, not a stitch of clothing on, tits unbound, pussy uncovered, and I'm about two seconds away from getting my cock inside her.

"Good." I whip my shirt off and undo the snap buttons of my jeans. My cock is out, hitting my abdomen. "Your choice. You want it from behind or face to face." I give her the option knowing how much she loves to ride my dick.

"From behind, your arm banding around my breasts, your fingers playing with my clit, that's how I want it." She's not drunk at all right now, probably buzzed, which is going to make this all the more enjoyable.

"Then come on." I guide her until her back is to my front and her legs are on the outside of mine. "Take my cock and guide me in." Pure bliss, that's what it feels like when she takes my cock, wrapping her fist around it, the way she bathes the head of my length in her slickness. My eyes drop to her ass, watching the flex and pull of the muscles in her body.

"Oh God, you feel so good, Nix, so fucking good." Her head drops back. My lips brush to her ear, teeth nipping at the lobe.

"Fuck yeah. Work my cock with your pussy, Leigh." She bottoms out. My hands grip the cheeks of her ass, pulling them outward, trying to get deeper inside her.

"I'm not going to last long," she purrs.

"Neither am I. Work your clit, sweetheart." She clenches down on my cock, her body locking tightly. I am guiding her up and down, lifting my hips when she is going up. We work together, reaching our orgasm together.

"Oh God, Nix." Head tipping back, a long moan leaving her, she shivers in my arms, and I feel her pussy shudder, pulling me along with her. My cum jetting into her tightness.

"Fuck yeah, milk my cock." The aftershocks of her coming are still wrapping around me. We're both slick with sweat, and the windows in the truck are fogged up. Marking this off as one of her firsts, it being with me, settles deep in my bones that waiting for Rosaleigh was worth it. I would have waited however long when it comes to the woman in my arms.

"You think you got me pregnant this time?" Leigh asks as she settles back in my arms. I don't answer at first. I'm happy as fuck she isn't pissed because I didn't even ask where I was coming, not that she knew I searched for her birth control. "I know you took matters into your own hands. I'm not upset. You did kind of give it away, not allowing me to swallow once, staying planted inside me long after we came."

"Every time I come inside you, I hope you are. It's a little soon yet. We'll know by next month, right?" I tip her chin up and to the side. My mouth lavishes hers, tongue tangling with hers, while my cock is still inside her, clearly not getting the memo that he's already got his. We'll be heading home soon, but for now, Leigh is content in my arms with my mouth on hers, and that's where she'll always be.

27

ROSALEIGH

"Why is everyone so chipper this morning?" I walk out of the bedroom, tightening my robe. Last night was the absolute best. After I confronted Nix about the lack of condoms and asking if I were on birth control, we stayed snuggled together in his truck until his cock finally lost its hardness, which meant I also lost him. It wasn't long after that we both got dressed, I climbed back in my seat, and Nix headed home, which is when I promptly fell asleep. The wine, the amazing sex, and the beginning of the best birthday ever lulled me into a deep slumber. I only woke when Nix placed me in bed and took off my shoes. He was going to let me sleep, but I needed a shower, desperately. I was sticky between my legs, and my makeup was surely destroyed. I pulled Nix into the bathroom with me, where we made love again. This time, neither of us said a word; everything that needed to be said was told through our eyes.

"Finally, the birthday girl graces us with her presence." I rub the sleep out of my eyes. Everyone is in the kitchen— Nix, Rory, Emmy, Ophelia, Ya-Ya, Papou, Conrad, and Sherry. My family is here. It doesn't matter that I'm divorcing David; that doesn't mean I'm divorcing his parents. Our children need them as much as they need the girls.

"Happy Birthday, Mamma Bear." Emmy rushes towards me, full steam ahead, making me brace for impact. She leaps, and I wrap her up in my arms, holding her tightly.

"Happy Birthday. We were going to wake you up, but Aunt Fif said you'd need the rest after your dinner." Rory joins on our hug, and then there's Nix, eyes locked on mine as he saunters over to where the girls and I are standing, hugging one another.

"Happy Birthday, sweetheart. Hope you don't mind having a houseful of people this early in the morning." He comes up behind me, big muscular arms wrapping around the three of us, whispering in my ear. Tears form in my eyes, and everyone and everything becomes a blur.

"This is the best birthday a girl could ever ask for," I respond, voice thick with emotion. The girls let go first. Nix stays wrapped around me, walking me toward our family, body bracketed to mine, intent on not letting me go, even when Ya-Ya makes her way over with Sherry in tow.

"Love you. I'm going to get started on breakfast. Fif has the drinks going, the girls are on the waffles, and I'm doing the meat, sausage and bacon. Dad has the eggs, and Conrad brought that syrup and hot honey you love so much. All you have to do is sit and hang with everyone. Let us take care of you, okay?" He kisses my temple, squeezes me one last time.

"Thanks, Nix." I have no other words, not in front of everyone at least. A girl needs to keep a few things private, like how she's so completely in love with the man she was always meant to be with, even if it took years down the road, how she wants to thank him in the best way possible, away from prying ears and eyes, namely Rory's and Emmy's, and how she cleared half the closet and dresser for his things, including half the drawers in the bathroom.

"My sweet baby girl, give me a hug, then go to my Ophelia before she complains non-stop that we're hoarding all of your attention. Plus, I think Sherry wouldn't mind having a word with you." Ya-Ya kisses my cheek. I do the same, hugging her close to my body.

"I love you, Ya-Ya. Thank you for giving me more than I ever hoped and dreamed for." I breathe her in. Nothing has changed, the jasmine and orange blossom scent, her perfume that she's never without.

"I love you, Rosaleigh. Happy Birthday." Then she's off, ready to tell everyone what to cook, when to cook, and how to cook it. Then she'll make sure the kitchen is cleaner than when everyone arrived.

"Happy Birthday, Leigh." Sherry is hesitant. We haven't had a moment to clear the air, the fact that I've got the paperwork rolling. I love my Emmy girl, but she did not think when she blurted out that her mom was filing for a much-needed divorce. Those were her exact words, or what Rory told me one afternoon after I came home from work, when Conrad and Sherry were helping out like the grandparents they are.

"Thank you. I know we probably shouldn't be talking about this right now, but there's no way I'm going to let this cloud hang over us. Rory told me that Emmy gave you the news. I would have preferred it came from me. The girl and her lack of filter will one day get her into loads of trouble," I try to make a joke to lighten the mood.

"I know. You should have seen her face when Emmy realized what she said. I don't fault you. You've given your life to David even when he turned his back on you. That isn't how you're wired. Instead of collapsing in defeat, you rose above it, busted your ass for your girls. Nix and the Drakos rallied for you, not that you needed it, and I'd like to say we picked up where we could even when we were unsure of our boundaries. I just want to say that I'm proud of you. I haven't said it enough, but you're doing an amazing job." It's me who goes to her this time, hugging her to me, unsure if I need it or she does, or maybe it's the both of us. It has to be hard knowing the son you raised turned out to be everything you never expected, to attempt to hold your head up when it seems like the world is throwing stones at you. I mean, sure, I had the same judgment cast, but unconditional love was not expected of me for David after doing what he did. If it came to my girls, and they did something like this, I'd still love them. I'd also visit them behind bars.

"Thank you. I'm divorcing David; I'm not divorcing his parents or his family. You and Conrad will always be welcome. It doesn't matter what happens—Nix moving in, a marriage, or a birth. You are always welcome. I think you know that judging by the fact that this is an impromptu party and he's wheeled and dealed the grandpas to work in the kitchen." She laughs at that last part, then a sigh of relief hits her. Sherry and Conrad have been in our lives forever. I don't see that changing, ever.

"My David never deserved you. I'm glad Phoenix stepped up. He's the best man for you and my granddaughters. Thank you for this talk. It's your birthday; you didn't have to do that. I appreciate it all the same. Now, I hear Ophelia has become quite the bartender, and we do have a standing obligation to try whatever she makes." Sherry loops her arm through mine and walks me toward the fray. I've still got two men in my life to say hello to along with a needy best friend. One I'd like to know how she's so bright-eyed and bushy-tailed.

"About time you get your ass over here. Now, mimosa or Bloody Mary, birthday girl?" I swear if I hadn't birthed Emmy myself, I'd have thought she came from Ophelia.

"Mimosa. You know how I feel about tomato juice. It is not the same as a tomato." You can't convince me that it doesn't taste like tomato soup mixed with some weird concoction. Plus the smell. Total buzz kill for me.

"One glass of champagne with a spritz of orange juice coming right up." Maybe it's a good thing Ophelia isn't at home often. I have a feeling my liver would not like me.

"Thanks. I'm going to go say good morning to Papou and Conrad." Before the girls were born, it was always Mr. and Mrs. Drakos, then it turned into the Greek name for grandmother and grandfather. Conrad and Sherry have always been their first names I've called them once David and I were married; otherwise, it was the same, using the James name.

"Better hurry up. Dad is already talking about how he's chopped liver these days. First the girls and now you. Tsk, tsk, bestie." I blow her off, grab the champagne flute, and make my rounds with the rest of my family. We may be a hodgepodge of sorts, but it's the best I could ever ask for.

28

NIX

"That movie was so good. Did you see how awesome the graphics were? I mean, wow." Emmy is talking a mile a minute as we make our way inside the house. It's been a few days since Rosaleigh's birthday, where she gave me a gift instead of the other way around. One that wasn't monetary but came from the heart —a place in their home for me to store my clothes, shoes, and the likes. Everything is still at my place tool wise, as are pictures I have from over the years, but I wasn't staying there much anyways. Rory and Emmy had no problem with me becoming a permanent fixture in their house. Little did they know it didn't matter the four walls that surrounded us. These three women are my home.

"See, I told you I'd pick out a good one." I've got my arm slung over Rory's shoulder. Emmy is walking backwards, and Rosaleigh is walking in front of us, looking over her shoulder, smiling happily. This week, her days off are separate, a freaking Tuesday and a Thursday. What the shit is that? I'm really going to have to work on getting Leigh to either find a new job, one that's Monday through Friday with an occasional Saturday, or persuade her to work at the shop for me. We wouldn't have to do a family movie night in the middle of the week, hurry the girls home, grab a bite to eat, and then head to the theatre.

"You got lucky," Rory responds. She was reluctant about seeing the science fiction film, much preferring a romantic comedy or replay of a movie that was older than even me.

"Are you agreeing that it was good?" I pull away and place my hand over my heart. Her eyes are dancing with laughter. Leigh is on the porch, ass to the railing, waiting until we all get closer to the door.

"I'm not saying yes, but I'm not saying no." Emmy bounds up ahead of us until she's standing beside Leigh, hip to hip. That's how tall she's gotten in the past six months. Rosaleigh isn't that tall to begin with. Rory is at eye level with her, and Emmy has a few more inches until she'll be the same.

"Can't admit when you're wrong and I'm right, I see." We take the last few steps, meeting them. The sun has long since set. Time change is a bitch when it's during the winter. Six o'clock at night, and it feels like it's nearly midnight. Shit doesn't get done as quickly; there's never enough time in the day. I'll be glad as fuck once spring hits.

"You do realize I am my mother's daughter, right?" I nod my head to Leigh. She takes Emmy with her, unlocking the door. No need in letting the heat out of the house while we're moseying along.

"There's no denying that. You and Emmy both. I see more and more of her in the two of you than ever these days. Minus the mascara." She pokes me in the side at the mention of her current obsession. When the girls came back from their visit with my parents, Rory had four new tubes of the shit, some weird eyelash separator thing, lip gloss, more clothes than I thought possible for what she had to spend, and while my parents don't mind spending money on them, I know for a fact they wouldn't overdo it. Emmy got two pairs of shoes and more clothes than Rory. Apparently, the thrift store was paydirt. Everything clothes was under a hundred dollars. The girls used their money and gift cards for the expensive shit, and the grandparents paid for the rest.

"Alright, get ready to wind down. Showers and homework. I don't mind which order, but get it done, please," Leigh tells the girls once we're in the house and the front door is shut.

"I'll shower first. All I have to do is reading." Emmy bounces down the hallway, leaving a path of clothes in her wake—shoes, beanie, scarf, and jacket. I mentally count down the seconds until I know Rosaleigh is going to remind her to pick up after herself.

"Emmy Lou James, if you want to keep your phone, you better pick up your stuff." Not even thirty seconds after her ten-year-old left it where she deemed it necessary.

"Yes, *Mother Gothel*." I hide my chuckle behind my fist.

"You got burned. She pulled out the villain from *Tangled* this time," Rory says. "I've got hours of homework. I'll grab a shower when I take a break. That way, I'll have hot water."

"I replaced the hot water heater today. You won't have to

worry about that anymore." I took the day off from the shop since Leigh was home. We loaded up in the truck, my mission getting to the hardware store. Two weeks of having hardly any hot water, and I was done. It was either the old thing was replaced, or I started taking showers at my house. Leigh didn't say a word through the whole process until it came time to pay. She attempted to slide her card, but I was quicker. Oh, she grumbled once we were in the truck. I silenced her with a kiss, then it was over.

"You're the absolute best! Have I mentioned that?" Leigh laughs at Rory. I walk over to her, now that the girls have gone their separate ways.

"You got a minute, sweetheart?" My hand goes to the back of her neck, massaging the muscles. One of her hands holds on to my forearm, keeping me there, the other settles on my chest right over my heart.

"I have all the time in the world for you, Phoenix." Fuck, I hope this doesn't backfire on me. The last time I offered her a job, she nearly took my head off, then listed every reason why we shouldn't work together.

"Now that things have settled down, you're not up to your eyeballs in debt, and the divorce is in the works, have you thought about finding another job?" I'm trying to feel her out to see if it's even an option for her. I know she doesn't mind her job. It's mindless which, hand to God, the woman is smart, maybe not with college math that Rory is taking, but she's too fucking brilliant of a person to be stuck in a dead-end job.

"Not really. I mean I should. I've thought about before there was an us, you know? Then it was put on the back burner. Do you think it's smart before the divorce is grant-ed?" At least she's thought about it, giving me an inkling of hope that she won't be opposed to a new job.

"We can always call Mr. McCallister and ask. I'm pretty sure there won't be an issue. You won't have to go before a judge. There's no parenting plan or sharing of a household budget. I do have an ulterior motive for asking. You know the shop doesn't have an assistant since Sophie was fired. Fif has been picking up the slack when she's home. The last time she was here, I was threatened that if I didn't find a replace-ment, she'd send Mom in to help." Needless to say, it did make Ophelia stay an extra day. What I wasn't prepared for was the heart eyes she and Eli had for one another. I left the shop for the day, working more the next day after she was back in California and the office was back to being clean.

"Fif pulled out the big guns, huh? I can't say that I blame her. Your office is a nightmare. Why you still use paper instead of going digital, I still don't understand." I'm about to pull out the woe-is-me card and really go for it. Leigh may see right through my shit; it's still worth a shot.

"Yeah, the software is there. I don't have a whole lot of time to get it started, train the guys, and still work on cars," I plead my case. Her eyes narrow. I'm so busted. I'm just hoping that it works. I'd love nothing more than to know my woman has a good job, one with benefits, rather than having to work in the elements. And we'd have about the same hours, too.

"Nix, if you want me to work at the shop, all you have to do is ask." Every time I turn around, ready to gear up for a debate, Rosaleigh does this.

"Fine. Rosaleigh, would you please accept a job as the assistant at the shop? It comes with holiday pay, health, dental, and life insurance. You'll have set hours, and I happen to know the boss can work around your schedule," I try to talk the position up, even with the look on her face that's telling me she's up for the job.

"Fine, twist my arm. Honestly, I still want to talk to Mr. McCallister first. If he says to wait until the divorce papers are signed, I'll do what he suggests. You're not the only one who doesn't like the hours at the nursery. The girls hate it. And now, having two separate days off in the middle of the week. It sucks," she replies. I'm only half paying attention because the view I have from where we're standing has my body locking tightly. My hand on Rosaleigh's neck tightens, causing her to turn to look around, too.

"Check on the girls, then grab your phone and meet me outside, yeah?" Telling Leigh to stay inside would add fuel to the fire, and something tells me she needs to be present for this shit.

29

ROSALEIGH

"I sn't this cute. She files for divorce to make a new family with my best friend," is what I'm greeted with when I walk out the front door, hitting the pound button on the keypad to lock the girls inside in case their own father decides to try anything. Nix was afraid David would make an appearance at some point. Given my penchant for not locking windows or doors, he replaced the front door and back door locks. I thought it was overkill, but it clearly wasn't. It turned out to be a necessity. Even the damn annoying locks on the windows; they couldn't even be opened except an inch, and even then, Nix made sure all of the windows were closed and locked as well as the doors each night as he shut down the house.

"Ex-best friend. We ain't been friends since the day you fucked Leigh over. If you have something to say, say it. If not, I'll give you a minute before I'm calling the cops. I don't want your girls to witness their father being arrested, but I'll be damned if you're gonna come to their house and start shit." I walk down the front porch steps, phone in hand, realizing too late that I forgot my jacket and I'm wearing my good house shoes when I know they'll get ruined. My mind wasn't on anything else except making sure my girls were none the wiser, I had my phone, and to get to Nix before it was him I'd be bailing out of jail tonight.

"Funny. I'm pretty sure those girls you're talking about are mine. It wasn't you who got with Rosa. You didn't have enough balls to go after what you wanted. That was all me. How do my leftovers taste, knowing it was me who took her away from you?" Nix doesn't say a word. He lets David ramble on and on as I make my way closer to the man who truly has my whole heart. The minute my hand slides into Phoenix's, some of the tension leaves his body.

"Why are you here, David? You left our girls when I was at work, left me to deal with the aftermath, and our girls with it, too. Do you know the hell we were put through? Or your parents? My God. Your parents aged twenty years overnight when we were told that the man we loved was a dirty cop, in bed with the cartel." How a small-town cop even figured out how to associate with some cartel in the northern part of the state, I have no idea, and believe me, I tried to work the puzzle out multiple times in my head. A piece of you thinks there's a reason for a person to do this. Was it you? Was it the life you created? Were you not good enough? If I were that woman who had a shopping problem or had to dress or look a certain way, sure. That's not who I am, though. This small-town life is all I've ever wanted. A sense of community with the family you love, it's all anyone like myself could ever want. Especially when you had a childhood as rocky as mine.

"I'm not staying. Not on your life. I knew Phoenix would swoop in and save the day. It was only a matter of time. You see, I knew he wanted you all the way back then, but he wasn't man enough to make his move. It didn't take much to weasel my way in, poke a few holes in the condom and getting you pregnant," David boasts. My mouth is hanging open, and a gasp leaves my mouth. And Nix, well, Nix has a grumble leaving him, a cross between a growl and an 'I'm going to kick your nose into the back of your skull.' I'm pretty sure if I weren't by his side and the girls weren't in the house, Phoenix would let loose. David would lose, too. Phoenix works out. He's not a gym type of guy, but he'll lift weights in his garage and runs a couple of miles a day. An activity Rory took up even though she abhors the thought of waking up earlier than she has to. Neither of them talk, they both run with their earbuds in, music blasting. Rory comes back home happier, and Nix comes back ready to take me as soon as the house clears out. The same can't be said for David. He once kept himself in shape, but now his hair is a greasy mess, his cheeks are ruddy in the type of way that you know his health isn't what it was, and he's got a paunch around his waist. He's not the same man, obviously, especially after spewing what he did to us.

"A predator, that's what you are. She was fucking fifteen, man. We were both older. There's this thing called statutory rape. You're fucking lucky she had a dumb-as-fuck mom, because it took everything my mom and sister had to hold my father and me back from beating you with a baseball bat.

Instead, we sat on the sidelines because Leigh wanted your child, said she'd make it work, loved you through it all. Man, you are one sick fuck." Phoenix pulls me back, away from David. Now would be the time to go ahead and call the police. The problem, though, is the girls would know. There would be no protecting them from watching their father have the officers he once worked with surrounding him. It was hard enough to shield them from the news reporters, as well as other agencies that have three-letter acronyms. They questioned me, and they questioned the girls, with me there, of course. With Papou and Nix hanging out right where we could see them, to step in if they got out of line. I felt like I was the one who took money and drugs that were seized instead of David with their line of questioning. You watch the movies, the television shows, but nothing prepares you for hours and hours of listening to them ask the same questions worded differently.

"I don't regret what you did. Does it suck that you felt the need to undermine Nix even though it was never that way between us? Yes. He was looking out for me while you weren't. David, you had it all. The two loving parents who doted on you, never having any problems growing up. Now here you are, in your thirties, creating problems because you can. Conrad and Sherry embody the value of unconditional love. I'll never understand what you did, and frankly, I don't care. What I care about are the two girls in the house and the man standing beside me. As for you, good luck." I don't ask why he's back, assuming the reasoning is he found the newspaper in which Mr. McCallister placed an announcement of the divorce. We tried to do it in another town, more populated, with a bigger newspaper population, but it wasn't allowed. If he were incarcerated, it would have been feasible, but with David being a fugitive, things were a bit tricky. It's also why it's taking longer. Two weeks may not seem like long to you, but it is to me. Mr. McCallister filed the paperwork, those damn acronym people along with the sheriff's office filed a motion, and here we freaking are.

I go to head back into the house. Nix is hot on my heels, protecting me from David yet again, placing himself in harm's way. I realize what Phoenix has been doing all along, shielding me and my girls. David is my past. Nix is my present as well as my future. What my future ex-husband did, taking that right away from me without consulting me to create Rory, hurts. You never regret having your children, no matter the time when you become a mother, not a womb donor like my own, who didn't even know who the father was. And while Nix took the decision off my shoulders, it was different. We talked about it. I'm not fifteen like I was back then. I could have put a stop to it, but I didn't and still don't want to.

"Cops are coming, Leigh. You wanna get inside and be with the girls quick-like, okay? I'm walking you to the door. I want all three of my girls to stay away from the windows. The cops are closing in. I'm going to stay out here. If you can, call his parents so they don't hear about it from the news." Nix and his supersonic hearing. The man can hear an ant crawling down the hall.

"Okay. Be safe. David isn't worth sitting beside him in a jail cell." Not that I'd let Nix do that. One call to his parents, and we'd all be down there beating on the door until they released him.

"No, the fuck he's not. I'm still gonna stay out here and make sure he doesn't do anything dumb. David's already done enough of that." I hit the code to the door. Nix waits until I'm inside, closing the door himself, essentially guarding us in the best way possible.

30

ROSALEIGH

"I called the cops," Rory tells me the minute I'm inside. She's sitting on the couch, phone in her hand, tears welling in her eyes. My baby girl, the one I raised while I was raising myself, the one who would lose her shit if I didn't rock her to sleep for each nap and each bedtime. Always so strong and courageous, calling law enforcement on her own father. She should have never had to do that.

"Oh, Rory Michelle, how I love you." I rush to her, not caring if she believes hugs are bullshit. I'm going to wrap my baby up in my arms, allow her to break down, to cry, to scream, to do any- and everything she has to in order to get it all out.

"Is it true what he said? Did he do that only because it was a game to him?" Son of a bitch. That motherfucker. If my daughter heard everything that came out of David's mouth, and now she's internalizing it and questioning her whole life, I'm going to storm out of this house and kick him square in the nuts. Nix won't be able to stop me either. Emmy walks out of the hallway around the same time I'm going to respond.

"Where's Nix? He didn't leave, right?" She's taking her earbuds out of her ears as she gets closer. My girls have some abandonment issues because of David and his epic failure at being a father. Now she's attached to Nix. Not that she wasn't before, but these days, it's more intentional, texting the group chat if his tracking app isn't working, making sure he's coming home when it's later than usual. Emmy and Rory both used to do the same thing to me, and now they've included Nix. I wondered if it annoyed him, especially if he was working on a vehicle. Nix being Nix shook his head and said, "The phone is for them to get ahold of me. They need to know I'm coming home and that I'm okay, you won't hear me complaining." The conversation ended, and I didn't bring it up again. Emmy looks at me, then at Rory, who's currently in my lap, sideways, face pressed into the crook of my neck, crying softly. I was hoping to at least shield one of the girls. My luck clearly ran out because Emmy is looking between the door and then to the two of us on the couch.

"Nix didn't leave. He'll be inside in a few minutes. Why don't you take a seat? It seems I've got some explaining to do." I open my arm, showing Emmy I've got enough room for both of my girls. She squeezes in, and Rory moves her feet, so she's tucked into a ball, my stomach taking the brunt of her knees.

"Dad's here, Em, and it's not pretty." Rory lifts her head, face red and splotchy. She uses the sleeve of her shirt to clean the tears as well as what I'm sure is snot, considering how wet my shoulder is, which means I also have it in my hair. The things you do for you kids, man.

"And we're inside why?" Finally, Em sits down beside me. My arm is around her shoulders, her fingers find mine, and she laces them together.

"Because Nix wouldn't have it any other way," I tell her, kissing the side of her head. "All I know is Rory called the cops, Nix figured they were on their way, and he walked me to the door and told me to stay put with his girls. I'm not entirely sure why your father is back, what he stands to gain, or why he's talking about what he is talking about. His problems are his own. Only he can fix them. Sadly, I don't think he's choosing to do so." God, it's hard to be the bigger person, to not admit what a dick David is. Now I get why Nix calls him Douchebag David. "That being said, if you want and the police gives you the opportunity, it's up to you if you'd like to see him." Rory's eyes nearly pop out of her head, like I had the audacity to bring up the conversation. One day, when she's a mother, she'll understand. But please let that be a long-ass time away. It doesn't go unnoticed by me that in two years from now, she'll be fifteen, the same age I was when I found out I was pregnant. Hopefully, my girls don't follow in my footsteps. Not that I won't love them. Damn, I don't want them to go down this hard-as-fuck road to get to the other side.

"No freaking way. I don't want anything to do with him. He's mean. What he did to you? What he did to us? And then to come back? I hope he rots in hell." Okay, hello turd in a punch bowl at a kid's birthday party, this is going over swell.

"You don't have to. I'm not making you. It was only a suggestion." I pull her closer to my body, hugging her so she can feel the warmth radiating off me, giving it to her in her time of need.

"The cops are here." Emmy flies off the couch and moves to the window. She didn't so much as give an answer. I'm not going to push it either. The red and blue lights are once again surrounding our house. I know Nix suggested I make the call to Sherry and Conrad, but there's no way I'll be doing that with the girls around. Rory's heard enough for a thirteen-year-old, especially if she heard the way her dad betrayed me to create her. I pull my phone out and shoot off a quick text. That'll have to do. I won't have to alert Ya-Ya or Papou. Our neighbor has probably made the call. They were friends of the Drakos when they lived here and are still friends to this day.

"Can you get away from the window, sweetheart, please?" I stand up, ready to rip her away if need be. Emmy moves but not toward me. She moves her body quickly, too, yanking open the door and going off in a sprint.

"Emmy, Emmy baby, stop, please stop!" I yell out for her, following in her footsteps. I swear if David hurts her, I'll be the one in jail, going down for murder, and I'll file my nails while sitting there, too, if it means he's out of our lives for good.

"Nix! Nix! Nix!" He spins around, ignoring the questioning of the police, his focus on Emmy and opening his arms as she leaps into his. I watch as her body quakes. Rory's stops abruptly, right along with me, hand finding mine. The girls may act like they're big and bad, with an independent streak a mile long. Can't imagine where they get that from. When it all comes down to it, the comforting touch we all give one another is sometimes all we need.

"You okay, sweetheart? I wish you had stayed inside with your mom. About gave me a damn heart attack, Emmy girl. That being said, any time you need me, you come to me. I'll always be here." Nix carries my baby girl in his arms as he walks to the bottom step on the front porch. The day is getting to me, because damn, all I want to do is crawl into his arms and fall apart like my daughter is.

"I love you, Nix," Emmy says between hiccups.

"I love you, Em. I love all of you." He holds Em to him with one arm, clearly understanding that we could use him as well, pulling the rest of his girls into him. Sure, there's chaos brewing around the four of us once again, but we wouldn't know. We're cocooned in our own world with the man I know now was always meant to be mine, who's loved me for as long as he's known me, and whom I'll love with all of my being for the rest of eternity.

31

NIX

"Okay, family talk time," Rosaleigh says two days later after the shit with Douchebag David died down. The fucker got cocky, coming back here to confront Leigh while also hitting some hiding spot where the rest of the drugs and money were. It seems David wasn't doing his job as a police officer, or what the cartel was paying for him to do. This was bigger than Abalee's sheriff's department. The Federal Bureau of Investigation was here, as well as the Drug Enforcement Agency. It was a shit show of a night, reminiscent of that night nearly a year ago but less intrusive this go-around.

"Oh God, you know what that means. Madre is doing the family meal planning, and I guarantee you it's going to be another sandwich," Emmy groans but throws herself in the stool beside me. Leigh is standing on the other side, a cup of coffee in her hand. Everyone is off for the week, me included, and I was the one who mandated it. No fucking way were we going to navigate dealing with a media circus.

"Har, har, har, Emmy Lou. Would you like a tuna sandwich or peanut butter and jelly?" Rory gags beside Leigh. The girl hates anything tuna out of the can. I'm the exact same way. The smell alone is enough to have me backing up.

"Neither. Nix will save us, and good. You just put your pen and paper away. The big guy and I will go grocery shopping instead." I quirk my eyebrow at her. Is she really trying to throw me under the bus, drive over my body, back up, and do it again? Emmy may not know it, but Leigh holds all the power. Rocking the boat is not on my radar. I sleep beside the woman. She likes my cock, and I love her cunt. Nope, I am not pissing her off.

"Mom, I'll eat whatever sandwich you make—fried, grilled, bacon, no bacon, tomato. I'll even eat onion on my dinner, but for the love of pizza, no tuna," Rory begs. Now, that I can get down with.

"I'm with Rory on this one. Em, you got some learning to do. That's not how you get on your mom's good side, unless, of course, you start helping in the kitchen more." I wink. My goal is to get Rory and Em both in here to help. No way do I want them moving out of the house and living on sandwiches, Ramen, and pizza.

"Okay, I hear you loud and clear. I do the best I can, you know. I don't see my two daughters coming to my rescue and helping cook or meal plan. Hell, I can't even get a request on what to have. You get what you get."

"And you don't throw a fit," we all finish together. My mother grew up telling us that. Now Leigh says it without thought. The girls laugh. Leigh has that soft smile on her face, content in how this morning is going as she takes a sip of her coffee. I think about how I woke her up. She was lying on her stomach, my body half on and half off hers. The soft whimper she made when I went to bring her closer. My cock was half hard, and there was no time like the present. Our bedroom door was shut, the alarm clock displayed seven o'clock in the morning, and I knew the girls wouldn't be up since they weren't going to school. A few movements later, my cock was slowly moving in and out of her tight, wet heat, and Rosaleigh was coming awake, realizing what I was doing. She was on her knees, the front of my thighs against the back of hers, feeling the way her pussy was clenching down on my length. Neither of us lasted long. The quiet breathlessness when we were finished was all the noise in the room.

"Alright, let me start the conversation. This isn't about food. We all know I cook most of the time, so a sandwich or two a week won't kill you. I'm pretty sure you eat that daily for lunch without a complaint." That puts the girls at a stop in their conversation. Leigh smiles proudly. I shake my head, a grin tugging at my lips as well. "You know the house is only a three-bedroom. We need something bigger. I'm going to marry your mom one day soon. Maybe she'll have another baby or two." I look at Em's open mouth and slack jaw. Rory's silently clapping. This is going smoother than I thought it would. "We'd like to move all of us into my house. Your mom always loved Ya-Ya's house and the memories she created there. The only problem is, it's the same size. If you two are okay with it, we're going to start remodeling, add a couple of bedrooms, a patio off the back, a pool since my yard is bigger."

"We didn't agree on that, Phoenix Drakos. Do you realize our house will be a revolving door of teenagers?" That, I didn't think about, though my home was like that growing up, and look who I ended up with in my life.

"Good, we can keep our eyes on the girls, not the other way around," I state, snagging her cup of coffee she placed on the counter. A few more weeks, and we'll find out if she's carrying my baby.

"Oh my God, a freaking pool. No way! Can we have pool parties, please, Mamacita, please next!" Emmy jumps out of the stool, hands clasped together in a begging manner.

"It's gonna be a bit. We're looking at six or seven months at the least. I've got no problem with it. No boys, though." I point my finger in her direction. Rosaleigh and Rory are laughing, knowing I'll cave the minute Em gives me her eyes. I'm fucking sunk when it comes to them.

"Does the remodel come with my own bathroom?" Rory asks. I look at Leigh. This part is her jurisdiction. I know for sure we're looking at four bedrooms at the bare minimum, along with two bathrooms, maybe three if we think it over again.

"You're lucky there will be a pool, just so were clear. We'll stay in this house during the renovation, and when the time comes, Nix and I will rent or sell this house. Are you sure you're okay with that?" Rosaleigh asks. We talked about it at length last night, as her body was lying on top of mine. I gave her the options when we first started talking about it. Leigh said the memories here were okay, but the best were made when she brought both of her babies home to Ya-Ya's. That's a family house, not the one that was shared with David.

"We're cool with it, right, Em?" Rory makes the statement.

"Totally. I'm going to go tell my friends that by the end of this year, we could have a pool. Peace out. Love you guys!" Em walks down the hall, furiously typing on her phone, alerting the masses.

"I'm going, too. A nap is calling my name. Great chat." Rory kisses my cheek, then does the same to Leigh.

"Well, that went well, but a pool? Really, Nix?" Rosaleigh isn't mad, more like shocked.

"Fuck yeah. You in a bikini and the water? I've got plans of my own when the girls are away." Heat blossoms across her chest. I knew she'd like that idea, and clearly, she does.

EPILOGUE
ROSALEIGH

Eight Months Later

A lot of things have changed in the past seven months, starting with my now pregnant belly. It seems we're destined for girls. At first, I was worried Nix would be disappointed because he already has Rory and Emmy, being in their lives for the entirety, that he felt like he was missing out on having a boy to teach his mechanic skills. I shouldn't have been surprised when he said, "Why? I've got girls in my life who can do it just as well as any man." Yep, he's a keeper. Another change is the ring on my very important finger. We couldn't wait any longer, as soon as the ink was dry on my divorce papers, made ten times easier now that David was transferred to an out-of-state prison where he's in solitary confinement to keep him

away from general population. Dirty cops flipping on a cartel
don't do well in there. I felt for Sherry and Conrad. It's
unimaginable to be in their shoes yet still loving their son.
We had a small wedding, with only our family surrounding
us, and when I say family, I mean Rory, Emmy, Ya-Ya, Papou,
Ophelia, Sherry, and Conrad. They had no problem showing
up. Nix didn't adopt my girls, though he said if the day ever
came when either one of them asked, he was all in. What we
did was make sure both of them were a part of our vows.

"Right there. Suck harder, Leigh. Use your teeth." I'm
sitting in my office chair. The blinds are closed, another
change for the better. Where most men would want their
women on their knees, no matter if there was carpet or not,
Nix would never allow that. Maybe in the bedroom, where a
pillow would go under my knees. Nix is protective, even
more so now that I'm pregnant. Which is why he's standing,
fingers tangling my hair as he thrusts his cock in and out of
my mouth while I keep up the suction. He's such a
gentleman that it was me on the desk a few minutes ago,
with him sitting where I am now as he took me over the edge
with my dress around my waist, panties stuffed in his pocket
as I rode his fingers while his tongue and mouth worked my
clit.

I turned in my notice to Minnie two point five seconds
after I arrived at work the first day back, offering to work my
last two weeks, but the media might be an issue. She let me
go on the spot. Yeah, our small town of Abalee didn't care too
much for hitting me while I was down. She then reached
back out and gave me a severance package a week later when
the usual customers noticed I wasn't at the nursery anymore,

making a fuss about how friendly I was and how the nursery was consistently open when I was there.

"Hmmm," I moan, scraping my bottom teeth along his skin as I pull back from his cock, taking a breath as I do so before sliding back down until he's completely seated inside my mouth. Nix is staying still as I swallow around his mushroom-shaped head.

"Fuck, I'm going to come, sweetheart. This time, you're going to swallow me. Don't let a drop go to waste." It seems now that I'm pregnant, Nix isn't particular about where he comes, spraying my body with his creamy white cum, coming inside my mouth, or when he's inside me. I don't respond. With my mouth full of his dick, it's near impossible.

"Leigh." The groan leaves him. He throws his head back, neck muscles working as I watch him attempt to hold back another noise in case we give away what we've been doing during our lunch hour. I've got news for Nix—everyone and their brother can put two and two together on what we've been doing. I swallow down each spurt as it shoots out of his body, trying to keep up with it so as not to spill a drop on my clothes. "Fuck, you look pretty, lips plump from sucking my cock, hair messed up from my fingers, clothes all jacked up because it was me giving my wife pleasure. Christ, sweetheart." Nix makes sure he uses the word *wife* as much as he possibly can to anyone who's willing to listen. Most of the time, I smile, but there are moments when I want to roll my eyes because it gets obnoxious after the first three times.

"Nix." I'm out of breath. His daughter is currently knocking the wind out of me, and I'm also recovering from giving him a blow job. I watch as Nix tucks his length back into his pants, his deft fingers working the buttons up easily, then I'm handing him the rest of the clothes we discarded. As for me, my hair is a lost cause, so I throw it up in a jaw clip, weaving it up, then down, securing it in a business-like look to go with my dress.

"Come out. I think it's time for lunch." He holds his hand out for me while my feet are finding my leather sandals.

"At least you aren't asking me to make you a sandwich," I grumble, getting hungry thinking about food. This baby is similar to my first two pregnancies—morning sickness for the first twelve weeks, barely awake and hugging the toilet, starving the second I smell food. Was there ever any guess that we weren't having a girl? Nope.

"I'd never. You're scary when it comes to food," he jokes. I smack his abdomen. He grabs my hand and brings it to his lips to kiss.

"Tell that to your daughter." We walk out the door after I finish cleaning up in the restroom, washing my hands, brushing my teeth, and making sure my boobs aren't popping out in their ever-present growing stage.

"She's growing. It can't be helped." I waddle along. The laughter that comes from Rory and Emmy when they see me coming down the hallway has us all laughing, which then has me rushing to the bathroom. Being pregnant is not for the faint of heart, or your bladder.

"You're as proud as a peacock, aren't you, Phoenix Drakos?" I ask, looking at Ophelia. Eli's got his arms wrapped around her waist. She's home now, but not in the house across the street from our newly renovated home. It's currently up for sale. Fif lives with Eli. They both found happiness. She doesn't live to work anymore, only taking jobs that she likes and won't take her out of town often.

"Fuck yeah, I am, Rosaleigh Drakos." I stop in my tracks. I'll never get tired of hearing Nix say my last name.

"I love you, Nix. Thank you so much for waiting on me." I attempt leaning up. Nix leans down so I'm not on the tips of my toes.

"I love you, Rosaleigh. You never have to thank me for being yours, sweetheart." His lips touch mine, a sweetness to him that he only shows to the people he loves, and damn, am I one lucky woman to know the feeling.

Want more Men in Charge? Staking His Claim, a small town brother's best friend romance is coming March 26th!

Amazon

Book 2 in the Men in Charge Series, Staking His Claim is now available

Amazon

Prologue

Ledger Sinclair, age 27

I never thought I'd be in the position I am now, my best friend is gone, way too soon, and way too fucking young, Montgomery Williams. The same age as me, childhood friends. Realizing they'll be no more dinners, no more sitting on the front porch shooting the shit while enjoying a beer at the end of a long as hell day.

How the hell this could happen, to a man as loyal as Mont, I've got not one damn clue. The call I received in the middle of the night jarred me awake, nothing good comes from the phone ringing at two o'clock in the morning. The person on the other end of line, Tulsa Rose, seventeen years old, a girl turning into a woman didn't speak a word. There's only three people on this earth who could have been calling me, Mont, Tulsa, or my mom, considering there was a shit ton of sniffling coming from the other end of the line. I knew. My stomach sunk to my feet. Neither of us said a word, feeling like I was about to be sick, I swung my legs over the edge of the bed one hand holding my cell to my ear, my forearm on my thigh, trying to gain my composure before making my next move. What seemed like a lifetime later when in fact it was only fifteen minutes, I was dressed, out the door, driving the few short minutes between my place and the Williams. The two cop cars were parked behind Tulsa's car, Mont's truck wasn't in his usual place, and the second I was out of my truck, long limbs running towards me, tears streaked down her face, hair flying behind, all I could do was brace for impact as she leapt into my arms, feeling her tears saturate me as Tulsa let loose. It was only once she fell asleep in my arms after hours of sobbing while I sat on the front porch steps that Judd and his dad told me what happened, Judd a friend of mine and Montgomery's, the other one his father that'd been on the force for years told me how it all went down. Mont was traveling home, when he was t-boned by a drunk driver, dead on impact, at that point I was holding tighter to Tulsa than I probably should have and it was me that had wetness coating my cheeks this time. Less than a week ago, the news shattered out world.

Today is the funeral and to say that things aren't going well would be putting it lightly, Tulsa has completely shut down, eyes downcast, body sunken in on itself, looking like she lost more weight than she can afford to lose. I can't say that I blame the girl. The Williams family has not had it easy, shit that comes in three's fucking suck, especially for the girl standing next to me.

"We're so sorry for your loss," those words are repeated over and over again at the graveside service we're currently having for Montgomery, his final resting space right beside his family in what is now a family plot in a cemetery here in our hometown.

"Thank you," I respond, Tulsa's body is leaning on mine, her hand goes from its place on my bicep down to my fingers, entwining our fingers together. A twitch in my body takes place at the wrong fucking time. Montgomery knew that Tulsa had no problem prancing in front of me, so close to being eighteen yet not, Tulsa assumed the looks she gave me was one-sided, it absolutely was not, and I had to talk myself out of so much as glancing in her direction when she would walk through the house in her bathing suit on her way to the pool at the Williams house. I curse myself at the feeling of her tits pressed against my arm. She's too young, gone through too damn much in her short life to be saddled with someone ten years older than her.

"Ledger," Tulsa squeezes my hand to get my attention.

"Yeah, Tulsa?" her head tips up slightly as mine lowers.

"I need to get out of here, it's too much," eyes that are usually a clear hazel color are now blood shot.

"Go ahead, I'll handle the rest of this. It shouldn't be too much longer," Tulsa wraps her arms around her frail body, making a mental not that I'm going to have to make sure she takes care of herself.

"Thanks," she nods before taking off, the black dress whips around her body with the wind, you can smell the precipitation in the air, a sure sign of the rain to start pouring down any moment now. Hopefully this will be wrapped up, we can head to the attorney's office, Tulsa can eat then finally get some damn sleep. And me, I can drown myself in a bottle, it doesn't matter what kind of bottle it is either, beer, tequila, vodka, whisky, or bourbon, all five would be good with me right about now. Anything to drown out the thoughts of how Montgomery is gone, and I'm left with the memory of how Tulsa and her firm little body feels against mine.

Tulsa Rose, age 17

If someone would have told me I'd lose three of the most

important people in my life within years of one another, I would have told you it's impossible. There's no way my mom would have passed away when I was only ten years old. A massive heart attack while dad was at work, I was at school, and my brother was away at college. My father greeting me at school in the middle of the day should have been a warning, the turmoil was written all over his face except I was young, not realizing what was going on, running towards him, a smile plastered on my face thinking he got off of work early and was treating me to a day away from school with ice cream. That wasn't the case and when he explained that he didn't hear from mom at her usual check in time around lunch, he had a weird feeling that something was wrong, he went home and found her unresponsive, it was only years later that I learned she died from a massive heart attack, two years later dad passed away in his sleep, from a broken heart.

Montgomery, God how I'm going to miss my big brother, he picked up the broken pieces of our life, he was already the brother, it was father and friend became wrapped up all in one who held the remainder of our family together and now I'm not going to ever get to have those talks over ice cream when a boy at school annoys me or when the time of the month hits, and the world feels like it's hitting me at every single angle. God, I could really use him right about now.

Instead I'm sitting of an attorney's office in town, Mr. Flay. Ledger is sitting beside me as we hear the final words of Montgomery's last will and testament.

"Tulsa, Ledger, hate like hell that I'm once again here with your family," Mr. Flay says looking at me.

"Yeah, I can't say that I blame you either," Ledger says to him, I've been quiet, lost in my own thoughts, worrying about everything that's going to happen from here on out, how I'm going to get through a single day, and I'll be honest contemplating it is a struggle.

"Ledger, you've been given guardianship to Tulsa Rose. Montgomery wants her to go to school in Alabama, the school she chose, and she'll be doing it as soon as possible, there's been money set aside for daily expenses, as well as on campus living. Ledger will be responsible of taking care of the family home while Tulsa is away," I gasp, appalled, how could Montgomery send me away, it's bad enough everyone else in our family has left me and now this, an imaginary knife twists inside my heart deeper.

"I'm not going to Alabama, I don't care what Montgomery says. I'll stay here and go to college," I stand up, feeling dizzy as I do, cussing myself black and blue because my appetite has been gone, not even toast is appealing.

"You're going to Alabama, you've been dreaming and working your whole damn life to get into that college. If this is what Mont wants, it's what you'll do," Ledger's voice is unlike I've ever heard before, deeper, darker, angrier. That's good because the feeling is entirely mutual.

"It's a good thing you're not the boss of me Ledger Sinclair," I mouth off, hands going to my hips, stomping my foot. I hate today, I hate all days, I hate Monday's, Wednesday's, and I especially hate Saturday's. But today, Tuesday might give the rest of the days I lost my family might just be the icing on the cake.

"I've got a piece of paper that says I am, so get over your

little snit. Why would you want to stay in this small town, you're seven freaking teen. I'll keep the house the way it's been until you've graduated college, spread your wings, live your life to the fullest. Montgomery didn't get that chance, and don't start, he never once begrudged anyone for that but he damn sure wanted to give you everything he could," Ledger says, I can't take it anymore, the world as I know it is no longer my own, I spin on my heels, running for the door, not ready to lose what little dignity I have left. I push the doors open with an energy I thought was long gone, my head stays down, the reception area is empty minus Leslie, Mr. Flay's secretary, even she doesn't say a word. I'm pretty sure this isn't her first time seeing people run away from their problems because that's exactly what I'm doing, the next door gives just as easily. The fresh air, the hot sun, the slight breeze it's what I need and it's all about to be taken away from me. Yes, I'm aware Alabama still has the same air, sun, and weather as Florida, it's not home, it's not Orange Blossom.

My ass hits the curb, the concrete hot and feeling good beneath my funeral dress, arms wrapping around my knees, head tipping to the side, the tears I thought were coming are suddenly bone dry, "You didn't have to run away Tulsa, we could have talked."

"Go away Ledger," I mutter, opening my eyes to look at him, soft wavy brown hair, chiseled jaw, angular nose, green eyes, a full beard that's short and trim, and the same dark circles match the ones I have beneath my own.

"Not happening, Come on, we've got some talking to do, butterfly," he calls me by a name I haven't heard him use in years, hand out and requesting me to take it in a quiet manner.

"I think it'd be better if talking wasn't necessary," his calloused hand slips in mine, engulfing me in more ways than one. Ledger helps me off the ground, pulling me into his body, allowing me to rest my head on his chest, arms going around his waist, I should hate him. He's so readily willing to push me away, and what do I do, I burrow into him further, breathing in his presence, a mix of leather, pine, and bergamot, a scent I've known for as long as I can remember. Any chance I could get to be near him, I took full advantage of, a hug hello, a wave here and there, I soon figured out he wasn't as immune to me as I once thought he was either.

"Spread your wings, Tulsa Rose, be the butterfly you were always meant to be, come home for the summer if you want or stay up there, it's entirely up to you. But you've got to do this, even if you hate me for driving you away," Ledger may be breaking my heart bit by bit, word by word, and I know one thing for certain, he's not as unaffected as he plays off to be. My body is flush against his, a presence against my stomach. There's no way it could be anything else than Ledger's length. Hard, clearly thick, girthy, and long judging by the way it's jutting upwards, and one day I'm going to make Ledger Sinclair regret the day he pushed me away.

Amazon

ABOUT THE AUTHOR

Tory Baker is a mom of two teenagers and a dog mom to one wild and active Weimaraner, Remi. She lives in a small coastal town on the east coast of sunny Florida. Oftentimes you'll find her outside soaking up the rays with at least three drinks surrounding her, a wandering imagination, and a notebook in hand where she's jotting down a plot for her next story. She's a lover of writing happily ever afters with Alpha heroes and sassy heroines.

Sign up to receive her **Newsletter** for all the latest news!

Tory Baker's Bombshells is where you see and hear all of the news first!

ALSO BY TORY BAKER

Playing His Games

Playing to Win

Vegas After Dark Series

All Night Long

Late Night Caller

One More Night

About Last Night

One Night Stand

Hart of Stone Family

Tease Me

Hold Me

Kiss Me

Please Me

Touch Me

Feel Me

Diamondback MC Second Gen.

Obsessive

Seductive

Addictive

Protective

Deceptive

Diamondback MC

Dirty

Wild

Bare

Wet

Filthy

Sinful

Wicked

Thick

Bad Boys of Texas

Harder

Bigger

Deeper

Hotter

Faster

Hot Shot Series

Fox

Cruz

Jax

Saint

Getting Dirty Series

Serviced (Book 1)

Primed (Book 2)

Licked (Book 3)

Hammered (Book 4)

Nighthawk Security

Never Letting Go (Easton and Cam's story)

Claiming Her (Book 1)

Craving More (Book 2)

Sticky Situations (Travis and Raelynn's story)

Needing Him (Book 3)

Only His (Book 4)

Carter Brothers Series

Just One Kiss

Just One Touch

Just One Promise

Finding Love Series

A Love Like Ours

A Love To Cherish

A Love That Lasts

Stand Alone Titles

Nailed

The Christmas Virgin

Taking Control

Unwrapping His Present

Tempting the Judge

Naughty Noelle

Hot Nights

ACKNOWLEDGMENTS

This is about to get very long and very wordy because that's just who I am. I've got so many people to thank and shout out that I hope no one is forgotten. When I set out about change this year, I was all freaking in. I'm extremely fortunate you all are taking this wild ride with me. The depth in these stories it fills my heart up with a joy I lost along the way and my cup couldn't runneth over without your support!

To my kids: A & A without you I'd be a shell of myself. You helped me find myself in a moment of darkness. Thank you for picking up the slack around the house while I was knee deep in this deadline, cooking, cleaning, and taking care of Remi (our big lug of a Weimaraner). I love you to infinity times infinity.

NaShara McClaeb: Ya'll can thank her for that gym scene in Staking His Claim. She still sends me so much inspiration, tells me when my sentences ar run-ons or incomplete. Gives me so much shit about y'all vs ya'll. It's ya'll for this girl by the way. There have been many a conversations we've had about a story. Every time I struggled, she was there to kick my ass into gear. I can't thank you enough! Also, she's my sports partner through and through

Katie Cadwallader (Okay Kyle it's Welter but iykyk): This woman right here is responsible for so freaking much and not just my amazing cover photos. We bounce off each other for ideas, she's the only person I know who is so creative and still have the mindset of a business consultant. Her family has become an extension of mine and I can't wait to see her again!

Mayra: My sprinting partner extraordinaire. Girlfriend, we made it through 2022 ahead of schedule. One day I will fly my butt to California to hug you!

Julia: How do you deal with me and my extra sprinkling of commas? The real MVP, the one who deals with my scatter-brained self, missing deadlines, rescheduling like crazy, and the person I live vicariously through social media.

Amie Vermaas Jones: Thank you for always and I do mean always helping me on my last minute shit. It never fails that I'm sending you an SOS asking for your eyes. Beach days are happening and SOON!

Thank you for being here, reading, not just my books but any Author's stories. We do appreciate you more than you know, the reason why we can live out our dream is for readers, bloggers, bookstagrammers, bookmakers, Authors, and everyone in between. THANK YOU!

All this to say, I am and will always be forever grateful, love you all!

Made in United States
Orlando, FL
05 July 2025

62654444R00154